QUEEN TITANIA

QUEEN TITANIA

BY

HJALMAR H. BOYESEN

Short Story Index Reprint Series

BOOKS FOR LIBRARIES PRESS
FREEPORT, NEW YORK

First Published 1881
Reprinted 1970

STANDARD BOOK NUMBER:
8369-3524-1

LIBRARY OF CONGRESS CATALOG CARD NUMBER:
77-122691

PRINTED IN THE UNITED STATES OF AMERICA

CONTENTS.

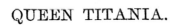

QUEEN TITANIA.

QUEEN TITANIA.

I.

Mr. Quintus Bodill, as had been intimated by his mother at the time when he made his *début* in existence, was an exceedingly handsome fellow. You observed at once that he was no crude *homo novus*, whose culture and polish are only skin-deep. There was something in the frank directness of his gaze, the soft modelling of his features, and the quiet and unconscious dignity of his demeanor which seemed to indicate a long transmission of inherited good-breeding. I would not say that his face was in anywise remarkable, except, perhaps, for its absolute purity and sweetness ; its innocence was at times almost touching, and yet, if you looked closely, you would detect amid all that blond and downy youthfulness a very definite hint of resolution and courage. The

3

passengers on board the *Melanesia,* however, were not sufficiently interested in Quintus Bodill's face to make these minute investigations. The absorbing topic at the time to which I refer—it was the seventh day from Queenstown—happened to be a funeral which had just occurred during the morning. A young Englishwoman, of the second cabin, had died the day before, leaving a four-year-old little daughter, who was just now being handed around and inspected by some officiously benevolent ladies. Quintus, who sat on a camp-stool, leaning against the gunwale, smoking reflectively, watched the distressed and frightened child with lively sympathy ; and thought of his own little sister at home, of whose appearance this bewildered waif remotely reminded him. What was to become of her? To whom did she now belong? Was there any one on the other side of the ocean awaiting her arrival? The wind whistled and sang in the cordage of the ship, the huge sail gave an occasional flap and again bulged out before the breeze, the waves rose with a rushing rhythm up to the very gunwale, then sank away with a wrathful hiss; and, down somewhere out of sight, the machinery kept laboring with a throbbing, nightmarish energy. But through it all the thought of the homeless and motherless child continued to haunt the warm-hearted Norseman. Presently he saw the captain—a shaggy naval bachelor, with terrific eyes and beard, and a voice like a bassoon—approaching the group of ladies who were temporarily interesting themselves in the little girl, and stretching out his arms to take her. But as he was stooping to her level, she gave a scream of terror, darted across the deck, and, sobbing, hid her face in the folds of Quintus's overcoat. He was quite startled at the suddenness of her motion, but soon began to find pleasure in the situation. He tried to lift her up on his lap, but she clung convulsively to his knee, and sobbed piteously when he bent down over her, spoke soothingly to her, and ran his fingers caressingly through her long, yellow ringlets.

All day long, with a wholly irrational devotion, the little girl followed at Quintus's heels like a little dog, and pursued him wherever he went. She sat on his lap at dinner, and would suffer no one else to come near her, and in the evening, when the stewardess came to take her away, she gave such a terrified shriek that he could not find it in his heart to part with her. He then retired with her into a corner of the saloon, and began to ask her questions about her father, mother, and her past life; but beyond the fact that her name was Tita, he could not coax from her a single item of intelligence. She answered, in a half-injured manner, " yes " to questions which mutually contradicted each other, making her father, for instance, simultaneously a resident of England, of America, and of heaven, and being apparently not in the least troubled by the inconsistencies of her testimony. It was very puzzling indeed, her face seemed to say, but she could not help it.

During the whole remainder of the voyage, Quintus and Tita were inseparable companions. From her elevated position on his arm, with her little, soft cheek pressed tightly

against his, and her chubby arms clasped
resolutely around his neck, she felt safe in de-
fying the whole world. She slept in the upper
berth in his state-room, and would never consent to close her eyes before he had seated
himself on the very uncomfortable ladder and
taken both her hands in his. She seemed in
everything to look upon him as the natural
substitute for her lost mother, and Quintus,
who was an absurdly tender-hearted fellow,
was so touched by her dependence upon him,
and so flattered, too, by her undisguised preference for him, that it hardly occurred to
him to throw off her yoke, or to rebel against
her despotic authority. He was perfectly well
aware that there were those among the passengers who were amusing themselves at
his expense, and he occasionally happened to
overhear remarks which made him marvel at
the possible baseness of human nature. Thus
he came very near having an unpleasant encounter with Sir Walter Thorndowne, who, in
Bodill's hearing, declared, between his yawns,
that he had no belief in disinterested gener-

osity, and that in all probability " the young polar bear " was more closely related to Tita than he cared to confess. On the other hand, Mr. Diggers, who had been canvassing Europe in the interest of some patent concern or other, and persisted in coming to lunch in a gorgeous dressing-gown, assured Mr. Bodill that he was delighted, by George! to make the acquaintance of a gentleman who had a heart under his waistcoat, and who was not afraid to take a hand where the odds were against him. He even carried his generosity so far as to propose to the captain that a subscription be taken up for the benefit of the child, pledging himself for thirty dollars, but refusing to head the list, because he knew that his plebeian name would prejudice the foreign passengers against the undertaking. The captain accepted this hint, and collected four hundred and fifty-five dollars for Tita, the sum to be deposited temporarily with the steam-ship company until it should be drawn by Tita herself, or by some one legally entitled to compensation for her support.

It was on a sunny morning in May, 186—, that the *Melanesia* cast anchor in the harbor of New York. Quintus was standing on deck, gazing with joyous expectation at the great city which was soon to receive him. He had half forgotten Tita, whom he was holding on his arm, and who, with an air of supreme contentment, kept rubbing her cheek against his, and occasionally pointing with delighted ejaculations at the queer men and women who were rushing about with bundles and boxes in their hands, gesticulating wildly and shouting in unknown tongues to the apathetic sailors and officers. The cabin passengers were already pressing forward to board the tug-boat, and a pang suddenly shot through Quintus's heart at the thought that the hour of parting was now at hand. Tita was to be placed in an orphan asylum in New York, the captain had told him, until some one claimed her, and if no one claimed her, she would be trained for a servant or a seamstress, or something of the sort, or perhaps be sent West, as soon as she would be able to shift for herself. Of her mother nothing definite could be ascertained, except that she came from London, and, under the name of Mrs. Marion Hulbert, had taken a second-cabin ticket for New York.

As Quintus stood sadly revolving these thoughts in his head, the captain (for whom Tita had an ineradicable aversion) made his appearance, accompanied by the stewardess, who held out her arms coaxingly to the child, promising her jelly, and making her all sorts of tempting proposals if she would come to her. But Tita was as much proof against bribes as she was against argument ; she only responded with a determined little pout, and clung the more closely to Bodill's neck. Quintus felt inexpressibly wretched ; he would have liked to yield to the impulse of his heart to take upon himself the responsibility for Tita's future. But what could he, a penniless bachelor of twenty, do with a child of four, and what sort of a future could he possibly prepare for her? With this reflection Quintus resolutely steeled his heart, and with a huge effort tremblingly unclasped Tita's tiny hands, which

yet clung about his neck with a desperate persistence. The stewardess, who was not troubled with much delicacy of feeling, hastened to
assist him, and with one rough wrench transferred the reluctant child to her own ample
embrace. Quintus seized his valise, which
was lying at his feet, and was about to make
his escape. From the bottom of his heart he
detested himself, and, in his innocent Norse
fashion, wondered whether God would ever
forgive him for thus basely deserting one of
His little ones. It was this thought, perhaps,
or possibly a mere natural impulse of pity,
which made him pause and turn about once
more. "Let me kiss you good-by, at least,
my child," he said, putting his arm around
Tita's neck and pressing her closely to him.
She looked so irresistibly lovely with the quiv-
ering little lips, the great tears in her eye-
lashes, and the air of profound injury in her
whole expression, that all Quintus's rational
reflections evaporated. The tears now came
faster and faster, and surrendering herself
completely to her grief, Tita sobbed on his

bosom as if her small heart was wounded beyond the possibility of repair.

"I want—to—do—with—you," she managed to say between her sobs. "I want to do with Twint."

"Oh, you precious child!" cried Bodill, feeling now no longer ashamed of his tears. "Yes, you shall go with Twint."

With heedless haste he rushed forward to the stairway, from which he boarded the tugboat. And there he stood, amid the wondering passengers, holding on his arm his tiny charge. He was not aware, this unsuspicious Quintus, what an amount of possible misery and bliss he was importing into the United States of America in the diminutive person of Tita.

II.

AFTER having left his prospective address at the steam-ship office, and satisfied the authorities that he was a proper person to be, at least temporarily, intrusted with the care of a child, Quintus betook himself with his charge to Jersey City, where a former groom of his father's, named Syvert Hanson, was said to be living. This Hanson had been one of Quintus's boyish admirations, on account of a rare and manly accomplishment he possessed of spitting through his teeth without the slightest movement of the lips. He had, however, vanished long ago from his friend's horizon ; but reports of his extraordinary prosperity had, from time to time, reached the family through Hanson's relatives, who took pains to convey the impression that Syvert was now as big a man as Colonel Bodill himself, and perhaps a little bigger. Quintus, who had been accustomed to hear marvellous tales of America, and had a vague impression

13

that the common logic of human life was not applicable to republics, would, therefore, hardly have been surprised if he had been informed that Hanson was about to take up his residence in the White House. As it was, he counted mightily on the ex-groom's influence, and fully expected to be introduced by him into the best society of the city.

It was about two o'clock in the afternoon when, after a long and futile search, he found Hanson's cottage. Its architectural unpretentiousness was a little disappointing to Bodill, but he consoled himself with the reflection that, in all likelihood, the stability of the republic required that its greatest citizens should be conspicuous, not for vulgar luxury and show, but for stern simplicity and uprightness. The idea was certainly a beautiful one, and Hanson was worthy of all honor for adhering to it so rigidly. With a palpitating heart he approached the front door, deposited Tita, who had just waked up from a sound nap, on the steps, and proceeded to whip the dust off his shoes with his handkerchief. He then arranged his hair

hastily, took Tita by the hand, and rang the
door bell. A slatternly-looking blonde woman,
with a baby on her arm, opened the door and
asked him rather gruffly what he wanted. If
there was any patent he was pedling, she
would tell him beforehand that she had no
time to look at it. The young man answered,
with extreme deference, that he had nothing to
sell, but that he had letters to Mr. Hanson
from his relatives in Norway, and that he was
very desirous to deliver them in person. His
name was Quintus Bodill, and he had himself
had the pleasure of Mr. Hanson's acquaintance
in his childhood.

"Good Lord!" cried the woman, in Norwegian, hurriedly depositing the baby on the
floor and grasping Quintus by the hand, "are
you Quintus Bodill, Colonel Bodill's son?
How glad Syvert will be to see you! Walk in,
sir, walk in. Don't mind the looks of things,
please. The children have it all their own way
here in the morning. And this is your little
daughter, I suppose. And I, who didn't know
you were married even; and not Syvert either."

"I am not married," said Quintus, blushing to the edge of his hair.

"Ah!" exclaimed Mrs. Hanson, in a more subdued tone.

She looked at her visitor with a sort of blunt kindliness which would have been amusing to any one less finely organized than Quintus was. He writhed under her imputation, which was too subtle to allow of a defence; moreover he felt that by the embarrassment of his manner he was accumulating inferential evidence against himself.

"Tita is not my daughter," he managed at last to stammer, as he seated himself on a carpet-covered lounge of loud coloring. "I merely picked her up on the steamship——"

"Oh yes, yes; I understand," interrupted Mrs. Hanson, with a smile of undisguised skepticism. "She is a beautiful child anyway, and likely as not you are quite proud of her. Seems to me she features you consid'able."

Quintus, with a little superfluous show of dignity, rose to take his leave. She, however, entirely unconscious that she had given offence, urged him to stay to supper, as Syvert would then have returned. He yielded reluctantly, because he knew of nothing else to do; and learned from the intermittent conversation of the hostess during the next three hours that Mr. Hanson was not a member of the cabinet at Washington, nor even mayor of New York, but a box-maker for the great publishing firm of J. C. Dimpleton & Co., in the city. The republican simplicity of his household thus became less enigmatical. A vast edifice of heaven-scaling aspirations which Quintus had during the voyage been erecting on the basis of Hanson's hypothetical eminence now tumbled down over his head. He evidently had nothing to hope from Hanson except, perhaps, a kindly greeting and some practical advice, of which he was sadly in need.

About six o'clock Hanson arrived, and by his mere appearance made Bodill feel the utter absurdity of his expectations. He was, to be sure, an honest-looking man, rough and square-built, loud in his manners, and, on the whole, a very slight and perfectly intelligible

2

modification of the former groom, whom Quintus had admired twelve years ago for qualities which now no longer commanded his admiration. One conspicuous change, however,
seemed to have taken place in Hanson since
his transplanting into American soil—he had
learned to think. His vocabulary, though
neither choice nor abundant, was certainly
energetic and expressive, and indicated that
his thought, which formerly had rarely risen
above the sphere of the stable, had gained a
much wider range. He had, especially, very
definite opinions on politics, and expressed
with much confidence what he would have
done in a certain recent emergency, in case he
had been President, until Quintus, who in his
Norse simplicity was quite impressed by such
magnificent talk, began to wonder whether the
President might not have a personal grudge
against Hanson, since he so persistently neg-
lected to consult him. The latter, greatly encouraged by his guest's impressibility, now
began to patronize him more conspicuously,
promised him the benefit of his protection,

unfolded his plan for the conduct of the war
(which was then in progress), and aroused
again in Quintus's bosom all the expectations
to which he had, but a moment ago, bidden
a reluctant farewell. After all, Hanson might
be at the same time a box-maker, and an important personage in the republic. Very likely
that was the peculiarity of republics, that men,
after having been divested of the insignia of
office, returned to their former obscurity, with
a chance, however, of being again as suddenly
raised to the pinnacle of glory. Was not Cin-
cinnatus taken from the plough to be made dic-
tator of Rome? And President Lincoln, who
was then occupying the White House, had he
not been a rail-splitter? Why might not a
box-maker, then, be suddenly called from his
boxes and charged to organize a cabinet?
Hanson promptly rose to his former eminence
in Quintus's estimation, and he was not a little pleased when the great man proposed to
him that he and Tita should take, at a moderate rent, the two spare rooms upstairs, which
had recently been furnished for the purpose of

accommodating a lodger. Mrs. Hanson promised to look after the little girl while Mr. Bodill was at his business, and considering the
old friendship of the families (old Colonel Bodill ought to have heard that remark, Quintus
reflected, smiling), she would charge but a trifle
for her extra trouble. The bargain was readily concluded, and the two European innocents
were immediately installed in their new abode.

The next day Mr. Hanson proved the value
of his protection by introducing Quintus to
his employer, Mr. Dimpleton, who seemed to
be greatly pleased with the young Norseman's
appearance, and, after some parley, engaged
him at a salary of forty dollars a month as
clerk in his wholesale department. The same
evening Quintus wrote a jubilant letter to the
family at home, in which he declared that he
had mounted the lowest round of the ladder of
fortune, and that he had now a fair chance of becoming anything except President of the United
States, from which office his foreign birth ex-
cluded him—a fact which he greatly regretted.

About Tita, however, he did not write a word.

III.

THE first four years of Bodill's sojourn in the land of liberty were extremely uneventful. His time was chiefly occupied in writing business letters, and in becoming Americanized, which latter process is, to be sure, not a conscious act, but a slow psychological fermentation which gradually changes one's original Old World substance into something rich and new and strange. Quintus, at all events, was satisfied that his metamorphosed self, at the end of the four years, was a finer and more valuable article than the primitive Norse self, which he brought over in the *Melanesia.* He looked back with supreme pity upon the *naïve* notions of the world which he then entertained, smiled at his exalted opinions of Hanson (whose patronage he now received with good-humored *persiflage*), and, on the whole, treated the still surviving remnant of his Norse personality as a younger and slightly weak-minded

21

brother who stood in constant need of his superior protection and counsel.

To Tita, on the other hand, the first years of her transatlantic existence were crowded with important events. In the first place, she displayed a singular tenacity of purpose in outgrowing, every five or six months, her frocks, her shoes, and her stockings, not to speak of those little garments which (according to feminine notions) have to be embroidered all over, even though they are never meant to be seen; and Mrs. Hanson, who understood that she had *carte-blanche* in providing for Tita's wardrobe, indulged her taste for finery to an extent which sometimes made Quintus groan, and would have betrayed him into the use of energetic language, if he had not been the kindest and most good-natured of men. However, Tita was so daintily made,—so soft and sweet and dimpled,—that nothing could really be too good for her. Her vanity ought not to be encouraged, he would often reason: and the next day, very likely, he paid for a blue silk sash, or a plumed hat (which was miraculously becom-

ing), or a lace-covered little parasol, fit for
Queen Titania to carry. What wonder, then,
that Tita was well satisfied with the American
republic! Yet, to do her justice, there were
other things which she valued more highly
than ornamental millinery. She always had a
vehement kiss and embrace for Quintus every
evening when he returned from his business,
and she could never be induced by Mrs. Hanson to close her eyes before Quint had presented himself at her bed and had submitted to
being smothered with caresses. Then there
was inevitably a little story with a pointed
moral, whereupon followed a long and affectionate coaxing for another, and still another,
until the long, dark lashes began to droop, and
the obedient squirrel children, and the naughty
fairy who received such summary punishment,
and the refractory little bird that found such a
tragic end under the cat's claw, all joined in
a confused procession, underwent queer trans-
formations, and hovered away into dreamland.

I am extremely sorry to record the fact that
Tita sometimes was naughty. She had, not

infrequently, violent disputes with Syvert Hanson, Jr., a young man of her own age, and if he did not yield to persuasion, she would adopt more serious measures, as, for instance, boxing his ears or pulling his hair. Mrs. Hanson would then interfere in her son's behalf, and the slate which hung over Quintus's desk would then in the evening contain the sad record of Tita's misdemeanors. On such evenings there were no story and no "good-night kiss," even though it nearly broke Quintus's heart to hear Tita calling him with a voice that gradually grew feebler as she sobbed herself to sleep. It occurred to her one day, when her conscience was not quite at ease, to break the "misdemeanor slate," which she regarded as the cause of all her sufferings; but it is needless to say that the ingenuity of Mrs. Hanson soon provided another. Poor Tita, how she suffered during the long hours of suspense while she stood weeping at the door listening for Quint's well-known footsteps in the hall! And with what remorseful tenderness she flung herself upon his neck as he entered,

and confessed all her misdoings, anxious only
to forestall the testimony of the dreadful slate.
Quintus, then, in spite of his stern resolu-
tions to the contrary, would gradually relent,
and, while half-unconsciously returning her caresses, would wring her little heart by his
sham grief over her monstrous wickedness. For
all that, it must not be supposed that Quintus
failed to realize the gravity of the task he had
undertaken in becoming responsible for Tita's
education. If he erred at all, it was on the
side of over-conscientiousness. He read Spencer, Pestalozzi, and even Kant's "Critique of
Pure Reason," with sole reference to Tita's
misdemeanors; he listened gravely, and with
a sincere desire to be enlightened, to the lec-
tures of reforming monomaniacs, and he even
began a system of severe self-scrutiny, hoping,
by constant watchfulness of his every thought
and act, to become, in time, a worthy example
to his ward.

Curiously enough, it never occurred to Quintus that Tita was educating him quite as much
as he was educating Tita. She gave, by her

dependence upon him, a value to his life which
it had never possessed before. At home, as
one of twelve children, he had never flattered
himself that he was of much account. He
knew perfectly well that he could easily be
spared, and that his parents (even though
they loved him very sincerely) must find some
compensation for his loss in the fact that his
departure to seek his fortune in the New
World had created a vacancy at their intermi-
nable dinner-table. He had never distinguished
himself either in school or in college, except
on a single occasion when he took a prize in,
Greek; and he had become thoroughly convinced that he was a mere average mortal, who,
as his name indicated, had no other mission in
the world than to figure numerically in the
census. Now fate had attached another life to
his, and accordingly, without reflecting much
about it, he rose perceptibly in his own estimation. All his thoughts and aspirations centred in Tita. If he had a new coat made, he
enjoyed beforehand the pleasure she would
take in watching him from the window as he

stalked up the street, conscious of his good
appearance, and he would smile a very affectionate smile to himself and puzzle his tailor
as he was just shouting out the numbers of his
measure. If sometimes, in crossing the ferry,
he saw a vision of wealth and glory unfolding
itself in the wintry sky, it was Tita, and always
Tita, who was to benefit by his greatness; it
was Tita who was to shine in silks and satins
and have the great aristocratic world at her
feet; and he—well, he would stand behind
Tita's chair and smile and feel happy in her
splendor. On Saturday nights, when he was
always in the habit of bringing her some trifling present, he would run up the stairs like
a boy to receive her greeting, and she would,
with much laughter and coaxing, investigate
his pockets, one after another, while he always
feigned an exaggerated grief at having forgotten the accustomed gift; and when finally it
was found in some inconspicuous pocket, he
would pretend to be greatly surprised, while
she would dance triumphantly about him, and
hug him, and call him all manner of affection-

ate names. And Quintus felt so supremely happy that he snatched Tita up in his arms and whirled around the room with her like a mad-man. Nevertheless, as I have said, he never reflected upon what he would have been with-out Tita. The case seemed hardly suppos-able. Tita as an educator! How ridiculous!

IV.

QUINTUS remained nearly eleven years in the employ of the firm of J. C. Dimpleton & Co. before he made the acquaintance of the head of the house in any but his official capacity. Then a little incident happened which was fraught with greater consequences to Bodill than he ever had anticipated. A certain well-known Greek scholar, Professor P—— (more remarkable for his skill in concocting text-books than for real learning), was about to publish an edition of the orations of Demosthenes through the firm of Dimpleton & Co. A large package of proof-sheets, already revised by the editor, had to be opened by Quintus before being returned to the printer, and on casting a glance on the page he discovered what, according to the best authorities, was a false reading. He then began to investigate the text carefully, and found several other evidences of what he would call either ignorance or very careless editing.

29

Kindled with learned zeal, he seized the proof-sheets and walked rapidly to Mr. Dimpleton's private office, and asked for the privilege of a moment's conversation. Mr. Dimpleton, who was a solemn and somewhat pompous man, with close-trimmed gray side whiskers and a bald head, raised his eyes questioningly to the clerk and asked rather sharply what he wanted. Quintus explained briefly the mistakes he had discovered, and requested Mr. Dimpleton's permission to communicate with the editor, as in his opinion it was not consistent with the dignity of the firm to publish an unscholarly work. Mr. Dimpleton gazed for a moment in blank amazement at his employé.

"Do you mean to say, then," he said, after having recovered from his amazement, "that you know more about Demosthenes than the professor who has written this book?"

"That I cannot say; but he is evidently not acquainted with the latest criticisms and emendations of the text."

"Well, if you wish to communicate with him I have no objection; but I doubt if you will beat him as easily as you imagine. We have published a number of his text-books, and they have all sold well."

Quintus withdrew hastily, feeling for the first time in his life a sort of superior pity for Mr. Dimpleton, whom, in spite of his stately demeanor, he could not but regard as a man of crude taste and judgment. He was resolved at any rate to have the errors in the Greek text corrected, and accordingly sat down and wrote a plain and respectful letter to Professor P——, calling his attention to the latest works of German scholars, and, moreover, to some important articles bearing upon the subject in a recent number of a philological journal. The next day he received a telegram, thanking him for his suggestions, and requesting him to stop the stereotyping of the book until the text could be subjected to a second revision. This was very flattering to his scholarly pride, and he treated himself to a bottle of porter at luncheon, in recognition of his services to science and humanity. A man who at the age of thirty-one still read Homer and Demosthenes for pastime, and who at a pinch could even himself concoct a respectable Greek hexameter, was, after all, not to be sniffed at, he reflected, smilingly; he was, in all probability, somewhat above the average of his kind, and he justly deserved to lunch at seventy-five instead of fifty cents.

Quintus was in a radiant mood as he again seated himself at his desk, and began, half-mechanically, to open the letters which had arrived by the noon mail. He was so absorbed in his joyous meditations that he failed to observe that some one was approaching him from behind, and that a hand was placed on the back of his chair. Suddenly, at the sound of his name, he turned around and saw Mr. Dimpleton. The publisher seemed to have something on his conscience, and seated himself rather uneasily on a lounge inside the railing which bounded Quintus's domain.

" Mr. Bodill," he began, in his peculiar, constrained manner, in which there was, however, a vague intention of friendliness, " I was somewhat preoccupied yesterday morning when you spoke to me about the Greek text. I am afraid I gave you the impression that I wished to discourage your interest in the concerns of the firm. Such, I assure you, was not my intention."

"I was not discouraged, Mr. Dimpleton," replied Quintus, cheerfully. "My zeal for Greek is never easily discouraged. It is what saves my self-respect when I am inclined to be too modest in my estimate of myself. And Professor P——, as if he knew my weakness, has proven himself a subtle flatterer."

He handed his chief the telegram which he had just received, and gazed smilingly at his face while he read it.

"Very gratifying," murmured Mr. Dimpleton, "very gratifying indeed."

He took up his hat and stroked it three or four times with the sleeve of his coat.

"Speaking of Greek," he said, gazing critically at the inside of the hat, "it occurred to me that perhaps it might interest you to meet my daughter, who has, I believe, made quite a study of the Greek classics. At all events, if

3

you have no previous engagement, we shall expect you to dine with us to-night at seven o'clock."

Quintus was somewhat nonplussed by this unexpected proposition, but was careful to conceal his surprise.

"I shall be very happy," he said, " to make Miss Dimpleton's acquaintance."

"And remember, seven o'clock."

" I shall not forget."

After having despatched the business of the day, Quintus accordingly returned home by the ferry a little earlier than usual, made an elaborate toilet (which excited Tita immensely), and at the appointed hour rang the door-bell of a handsome house in Madison Avenue. The door was promptly flung open by a martial-looking negro in blue-and-yellow livery, who scanned him critically, and finally decided to permit him to enter. Quintus, who very opportunely remembered that the pedigree of the Bodills dated back to the earls of the ninth century, determined in his heart not to be dazzled, although (to be candid) the sombre magnificence of the parlor, with its enormous mirrors, its rich, dark curtains, its gilt-framed pictures and artistic decorations, was, to his innocent Norse eyes, marvellously impressive. A parlor had always, to him, signified a very simple arrangement of tables and chairs, inclosed within four walls; the chairs intended for sitting on, and the tables for depositing books, paper-cutters, and other stray objects upon. But this wonderful complexity of harmoniously blending lines and colors; this studied combination of effects in carpets, draperies, and in each separate group of furniture; this subdued and impressive *ensemble*—indeed the earls of the ninth century themselves would have felt for a moment stunned in Mr. Dimpleton's parlor.

Quintus somehow derived the impression that Miss Dimpleton, even though she did wear spectacles, and, possibly, short hair, was a lady of taste and refinement. His reflections, however, were cut short by the sudden consciousness that some one was approaching from one side. He turned quickly and saw a young lady, apparently not far advanced in the twenties, holding out her hand to him and bowing in gracious recognition of his greeting.

"I am very happy to meet you, Mr. Bodill," she said, motioning him to be seated.

"Have I the honor to speak with Miss Dimpleton?"

"Yes, you certainly have that honor," answered the young lady, with a frank laugh.

Quintus had somehow got the spectacles and the short hair so firmly associated with Miss Dimpleton's personality that he could hardly conceal his surprise at the agreeable disappointment. For Miss Dimpleton, though you would at first sight have pronounced her a sensible girl, about whom there was no nonsense, had nothing "emancipated" or unpleasantly aggressive in her manner or appearance; and yet it occurred to Bodill, as he sat looking quite guilelessly into her pure, handsome face, that she would have made a very nice boy. Especially were the large gray eyes expressive of a fearless candor which one associates rather with the male than with the female sex.

The distinctive feature of her face, however, was a fairly well-modelled mouth, about which there was a strangely conscious air. She moved her lips a little too much when she spoke, and always with a certain curious precision.

"And you are the disguised prince or viking," she was saying, as she seated herself opposite her guest, "whom father has kept concealed for years down in his store without communicating the fact to his family. Now tell me, how can a gentleman of your wild and fierce ancestry tolerate being chained to a writing-desk for so long a time? Don't your ancestral instincts sometimes awake in you? Don't you occasionally feel like breaking the furniture?"

"Our blood has been very much diluted and our type enfeebled and subdued during the last five or six centuries," he answered, with a pleasant laugh. "I am nothing but a degenerate late-comer, who am conscious of no heroic instincts whatever."

"In the matter of Greek, however, I am told that you have finely developed critical eyes—

a trait which, by the way, I should never have
expected in so close a relative of William the
Conqueror."

" Well, there, you see, you draw a rash conclusion. You, too, for aught you know, may
be a relative of some blood-thirsty Saxon bar-
barian, and yet you have an enthusiasm for
Homer which very likely would have been in-
comprehensible, even to your nearest kin, a
dozen generations back."

"Very likely. We have all kept pace in our
change of tastes and habits. Imagine, in case
we had met, say eight centuries ago, how different we should both have been, and how different our meeting. You would, of course,
have been a Norse viking, with long blond
hair, picturesque attire, and predatory habits.
I should have been—let me see--the daughter
of some Saxon thane, who sat with my maids
and spun the yellow flax the livelong day, and
only appeared in the parlor on state occasions.
Well, we will say that your arrival were such
an occasion, what do you suppose we should
have talked about ? "

" If I came with a peaceful purpose, I should
tell you of my adventures on sea and land ; but
if, as is more probable, I came intent on mis-
chief, I should carry you on board my ship
without consulting your wishes, and you
would be very sea-sick on the voyage to Norway."

" How dreadful ! " she cried, merrily. " How
fortunate that we did not meet in the eleventh
century ! "

" And who knows," he reflected smilingly,
" whether I may not do the very same thing in
the nineteenth." But aloud he said, while his
smile grew so irresistible that she could not
help joining, " Worse things may happen to
a woman than being carried away to Norway."

They were now fairly launched on a playful
discussion which had yet seriousness enough
in it to make it not wholly unprofitable. Then
Mr. and Mrs. Dimpleton appeared, just as the
butler pushed back the folding-doors to the
dining-room, displaying a table which appealed
to all Bodill's senses at once, except that of
hearing, this latter sense being kept steadily

and agreeably busy by Miss Dimpleton. It
required no great amount of insight to discover that she was the ruling genius of the
household ; for the quick way in which she
surveyed her father's toilet as he entered, and
then sent him an approving little nod, as much
as to say that he had done nobly, could only
be interpreted to mean that Mr. Dimpleton was
naturally too fond of undress, and subjected
himself to the inconvenience of frequent toilets
out of regard for his daughter's opinion.   The
butler, too, betrayed some little uneasiness as
she paused to take in the total effect of the
table, and was apparently relieved when, in the
next moment, she was smiling with evident
amusement at one of Bodill's remarks.

Mrs. Dimpleton was that deplorable American institution, the chronic invalid. She had
a pale and withered look, sighed frequently, as
if she thought that life was, after all, a weari-
some affair, and while speaking cast her eyes
in an aimless, wandering way up toward the
ceiling, as if she sought a solution there of the
troubles which perplexed her. She was small

and daintily made, and her features bore yet in them a faded memory of their beauty.

"Jessie tells me that you are such a great scholar, Mr. Bodill," she said, between two sips of the soup.

"Miss Dimpleton is very kind to say such pleasant things about me," he answered; "although I hope, for her sake, that the Recording Angel was off duty when she said it."

"You must pardon me if I don't quite understand you," sighed his hostess. "You must remember I am not learned at all, like you and Jessie."

"Mr. Bodill only hints that I have exaggerated his scholarship, mother," commented Miss Jessie, from the other side of the table.

"Now, speaking of scholarship," Mrs. Dimpleton went on, as the waiter was removing the soup-plates, "do you know Jessie there" (she lowered her voice to an almost confidential whisper), "reads and speaks Latin, and Greek, and Hebrew, and Gothic, and Anglo-Saxon, and I don't know how many other outlandish tongues. Her teacher, Mr. Schnabelstein, told me she was the greatest genius he had ever known. And only think of it, he was a German professor, and we paid him four dollars an hour. He even said that——"

"Mother, mother," interrupted Miss Jessie, laughingly, "I know by your expression that you are on your favorite theme. Please don't tell Mr. Bodill how that rogue Schnabelstein gave vent to his imagination as a preliminary to obtaining from you a loan of two hundred dollars. When Mr. Bodill finds out what a poor blunderer I am, I shall seem positively ridiculous to him, unless he has the kindness to forget Mr. Schnabelstein's insincere praises."

"Now, Mr. Bodill," the elder lady resumed, unmindful of her daughter's interruption, "that is the way she is all the time, whenever I say anything about her accomplishments. Of course I can't keep track of all the languages she learns, but I believe the last one she studied was the Croptic."

"The Croptic?" repeated Quintus, looking quite puzzled.

"Oh, mother!" cried the daughter, in mock

despair, in which there was, however, a note of real annoyance ; " I never studied the Croptic language, nor the Coptic either. Mr. Bodill," she continued, turning to Quintus, "my mother imagines that whenever I mention a thing I necessarily know it. The other day I was reading a French essay with some interesting references in it to the Copts, and, in endeavoring to tell the substance of it to a friend who was here the other evening, I evidently gave the impression to mother that I was studying Coptic."

Mr. Dimpleton, who during this conversation had maintained a severely neutral countenance, as if neither the Croptic nor the Coptic in the least concerned him, now raised his clean shaven chin out of his stiff cravat, and inquired, in a hushed and solemn voice, whether they had lobsters in Norway ? Mr. Bodill, although the abruptness of the question struck him as very ludicrous, replied gravely in the affirmative. "And were the Norwegian lobsters very good?" "They were excellent, thank you." "And did the natives of Norway dress in fur all

the year round?"   "No, they did not when they
went to bed, nor in the ballroom, nor, in fact,
on any other occasion, except in midwinter,
when they were travelling."   "What were the
staples of diet in Norway?"   "They were bread,
meat, fish, milk, very much as in the rest of the
civilized world"—all of which seemed very wonderful and surprising to Mr. Dimpleton.   Quintus was just beginning to feel like a wild man
of Borneo, or a polar bear escaped from a men-
agerie, when his host (as Quintus suspected,
at a hint from his daughter) took pity on him,
and suddenly ceased to exhibit his interest in
Norway.   He had, of course, been under the
impression that he was making himself very
agreeable, and if he had noticed the slight
look of annoyance in Miss Jessie's face, would
have been at a loss to account for it.

V.

FROM that day Bodill found his position in the house of J. C. Dimpleton & Co. entirely changed. From a simple clerk he became, in a sort of half-acknowledged way, the most trusted and confidential adviser of the firm. Manuscripts were continually submitted for his approval, and his judgment on them, if positively expressed, was always decisive. The firm never rejected what he strongly recommended, nor accepted for publication what he condemned. In the case of two or three venturesome undertakings which Mr. Dimpleton would not have touched if Mr. Bodill had not thrown his influence in their favor, the firm had an opportunity to submit his intelligence and his commercial sagacity to the crucial test; and as both prosperity and an increase of dignity resulted from the venture, it seemed obvious to the chief of the house that Mr. Bodill had now fairly earned his title to partner-

ship in the firm. The offer was accordingly
made on very favorable conditions, and, after
some hesitation on Bodill's part, accepted.
The thought had sometimes occurred to him
that it might be Miss Jessie's influence, rather
than his own merits, which had so rapidly advanced his fortunes, and he was too proud to
wish to be indebted to any one for so substantial a favor. He concluded, however, after
much meditation, that all Miss Jessie had
done was to furnish the opportunity, which he
had himself improved.

It is needless to say that he was all this time
a constant visitor at Mr. Dimpleton's house.
He had completely captivated Mrs. Dimpleton,
who was less languid and more confidential
with him than with any one else. He discovered, to his great amusement, that this innocent little lady had a decided taste for wicked
French novels, which she read without the
faintest suspicion of their impropriety. He
half divined that she was a little bit obtuse,
but he would not have thought it possible, if
his own ears had not convinced him, that any

one could read the books she read without sup-
plying what was left unexpressed in the text, or
comprehending a single one of the veiled allu-
sions. He also discovered (what was still more
amusing) that the daughter was, in a measure,
the guardian of her mother's morality; and,
indeed, Mrs. Dimpleton made no secret of the
fact that Miss Jessie hid away all the novels
which were procured without her permission,
or read them herself before allowing her
mother to see them.

"She is such a queer child," said Mrs. Dimpleton, taking it always for granted that her
listener was no less interested in this inex-
haustible theme than she was herself. "Now,
would you believe it, Mr. Bodill, when she was
a little girl of six she crept under the bed one
day, and lay there crying because she was not a
boy? And when she was only three years old,
she said the cutest things which ever I did
hear. She had come in in her little night-gown
to kiss me and her father and her uncle good-
night, and when she had gone the round once,
she insisted upon ' tissing papa adain,' and then

mamma once more, until I was afraid she was
catching cold, and carried her off by main
force to her nursery. Then I made her kneel
down beside her crib to say her prayers. But
the little midget was in a contrary mood, and
refused to utter a word. She was so stubborn
that I knew I should have to give in. So I told
her just to ask God to make Jessie a better
little girl, and she might go to bed. And what
do you think she did? Down she went on her
knees and prayed that Dod would make mamma
a better little mamma. Now, wasn't that bright
in a child of three? And I assure you she
wasn't ten years old before she began to correct
my pronunciation and to look after my clothes,
as if she had been my mother and not my
child."

It was chiefly his pleasant laugh, his unobtrusive politeness, and, above all, his talents
as a listener, which secured Quintus Mrs. Dimpleton's favor. To gain the approval of the
daughter, more pronounced qualities were required. Until she made his acquaintance, Miss
Jessie had had no very high regard for men.

Women were in all respects so much more adorable than men: they were attuned to a finer key. In accordance with this theory, Miss Jessie spent the first twenty-two years of her life in falling in love with women, and mostly with those whose attractions, to the coarse masculine vision, were imperceptible. A man, she had hitherto maintained, was only to be tolerated when he was instructive, and she had therefore selected her male acquaintance with sole reference to her own mental improvement. Quintus, too, she had sought on the same principle, because she desired to profit by his knowledge of Greek. And in this she was not disappointed. The Norseman, to whom this opportunity of refreshing the delightful impressions of his college days was very welcome, readily consented to a course of reading in Homer, and, from that time forth, spent every Thursday evening with Miss Dimpleton in Homeric discussion. Jessie began to reflect that a man was, after all, not such an objectionable phenomenon as she had imagined. She had never, even with her most adorable

4

female friends, had such a delicious sense of feeling herself completely understood. When Quintus recounted, with much delicacy of perception, the characteristics of the Greek civilization, or pointed to the occult and elusive beauties of the text, she could not quite suppress the thought that the daily companionship of such a man through a long united life was the very ideal of happiness of which she had dreamed.

When Quintus returned home about midnight from these Homeric diversions, he always found Tita cuddled up in a chair, wide-awake and excited. She was now sixteen years old, and had a room of her own on the other side of the hall, but she yet persisted in her childish habits, and refused to go to sleep without her good-night kiss. Quintus once, as a joke, sent her one in an envelope, before departing for Madison Avenue, and told her to go to bed like a sensible little girl; but when, on reaching home, he paused at her door to listen, he heard a sound of sobbing within. He was for a moment puzzled; then he knocked, but received no answer.

"Good-night, Tita dear," he said; "am I not to have my good-night kiss?"

The weeping ceased immediately within, and Tita's voice, with a little unnatural tremor in it, answered:

"You will find it on your writing-desk, inclosed in an envelope."

"She is a child yet, God bless her," murmured Quintus, with a sigh of relief, as he entered his study, and with a meditative smile opened Tita's note with the kiss duly inclosed. For better preservation, it was wrapped in red tissue-paper. The note read as follows:

"QUINTUS BODILL, Esq.:

"DEAR SIR :—Inclosed please find a good-night kiss from the undersigned.

"Yours truly,

"T. HULBERT."

That "T. Hulbert" was delicious. Quintus flung himself back in his chair, pressed the dear little note to his lips, and sat for half an hour smiling the kind of smile which is not irreconcilable with tear-suffused eyes. Tita's helpless and pathetic indignation reminded

him of the wrath of a canary-bird, which ruffles
up its feathers and pecks away fearlessly at
your fingers, imagining all the while that it is
inflicting a dreadful amount of damage. And
yet the comparison, in the next moment, struck
him as ungenerous. Tita's feelings, whether
they were wise or foolish, were certainly a
matter of great concern to him, and it was his
duty to exert himself to find out the cause
even of her strange caprices. That she, who
knew him so well, should take offence at an
innocent ·joke, seemed wholly incomprehen-
sible. That she objected to his Homeric evenings, and was possibly jealous of Miss Dimpleton, whose praises he had loudly spoken during
all the winter, was a thought which did not
even occur to him. For had she not, on a hundred other occasions, urged him to go to thea-
tres and clubs, and to call on friends, alleging
always that she was not at all lonely, but could
spend her evenings delightfully with her books?
Had she not always been the apple of his eye,
and was it possible that any one could ever
occupy her place in his affection? Ah, the

query was absurd. There was no place in his
heart for any one but her. And yet the possibility of his marrying Miss Dimpleton had
frequently been contemplated, and how could
he, as an honorable man, marry her without
giving her a place at Tita's side in his heart?
Somehow Miss Dimpleton, with her clear,
handsome face, and her bright eyes beaming
with intellectual enthusiasm, and the sweet,
golden-haired Tita, with her vehement affection and her naughty pout, made such a queer
contrast that he could not think of both in
harmonious juxtaposition as members of the
same household. Here was a problem which
would have puzzled the seven sages, provided
the seven sages ever were in love and were inclined to bestow their affections in equal divis-
ions upon equally charming women. Quintus,
feeling his utter inability to cope with so large
a question, resolved to temporize, and to allow
circumstances as wide a scope as possible in
shaping his destiny.

VI.

In spite of his liberal politics, Quintus was, like most Norsemen, a creature of habit. Although his income and position would long ago have warranted him in removing to a more fashionable locality, he postponed the evil day from year to year, always arguing that, until the time came for bringing Tita out in society, there was no cause for haste. He had reared her tenderly, guarding her from all evil influences, and he dreaded the day when she should pass beyond his control. For ten years he had devoted nearly every evening of his life to her education, and had seen with delight that his approbation was dear to her, and his praise the highest reward of effort. Beside the Hansons and the Norse families who visited there, she knew but few, and readily perceiving Quintus's superiority to those, she came to look upon him as the ideal of human perfection. She would not tolerate even an

54

implied criticism of his appearance or character, and Mrs. Hanson incurred her lasting
displeasure by remarking that he was greatly
to blame for keeping her so close, and giving
her so little pleasure. This very thought, however, had occurred to Bodill, too, one morning
as he was crossing the ferry, and he marvelled
at his own stupidity in not having thought of
it before. He resolved on the spot to procure
Tita a fitting toilet for the theatre, and to take
her as often as he could spare an evening to
accompany her. Perhaps she might also like
to drive in the Park; and if so, there was no
reason why she should not, when he was not
required at the office. Really, he had been
culpably thoughtless.

It was about a week after this resolution
was taken, that Tita, leaning on Quintus's arm,
entered Booth's Theatre, where Rignold was
at that time playing "Henry V." Her protector, who was as ignorant as a babe as to the
effect of millinery upon the female character,
was in a state of abject admiration and astonishment. He had always known that Tita was

beautiful, but he had never known that she was *so* beautiful. Like the peasant in the fairy tale, he had unwittingly been the foster-father of a princess. Tita discovered that night (what she had never been aware of before) that she possessed a rare talent—the talent for luxury. Poor Quintus, who was trembling lest he should step on something, or tear something, or in any way damage the elaborate effect, blushed with suppressed agitation, and vaguely wondered that the whole audience did not rise to its feet to contemplate Tita's magnificence. But, as far as he could observe, there was no one who was abnormally excited. He was, however, too absorbed in Tita to notice immediately two ladies in a box, not far away, both of whom had their opera-glasses levelled toward where he was sitting. Presently he became aware that some one was bowing to him, and while returning the salutation, he discovered that it was Miss Dimpleton and her mother. Then the thought flashed through his brain that, although he had been intimately acquainted with Miss Dimpleton for more than a year, he had never mentioned Tita's name to her. He had at first been restrained by a fear that she would look upon his adoption of this homeless waif as a quixotic and ridiculous act, and he knew that he had no tenderer spot in his heart, or one capable of being more cruelly wounded. Miss Dimpleton had in the first period of their acquaintance appeared to him as the personification of pure reason, and the apprehension seemed by no means ill-grounded that she might feel a pitying superiority to a man who was capable, on the spur of the moment, of performing an irrationally generous deed. When he had once established himself in her friendship, he discovered that he had done her injustice; but the very fact that he had delayed the revelation so long was sure to throw a false light upon it, and even arouse suspicion. With every month that passed, the original mistake became more difficult to remedy, and Bodill became conscious of a positive guilt whenever (as had often happened before the incident with the imprisoned kiss) his little girl came running toward him, greet-

ing him with outstretched arms and overwhelming him with her vehement caresses.

He moved a little uneasily in his seat as,
even after the curtain had risen, he became
conscious of Miss Dimpleton's continued
scrutiny. Tita apparently aroused her curiosity in an unusual degree. He began to imagine all the thoughts that must be passing
through her head,—her puzzled defence of his
integrity and her inability to harmonize his
various statements about his having no female
acquaintances, except herself, outside of his
home, with the presence of this striking young
lady at his side. The gorgeous pageants on
the stage followed in quick succession, but his
imagination went on an independent journey
of exploration and conjecture ; and when the
curtain rolled down over the last scene, he
could hardly remember a single phrase or incident. Tita, on the other hand, had been
immensely entertained. She acted the woo-
ing scene in Quintus's study after they got
home, and talked English with a French ac-
cent, à la Princess Catherine, for a week after.

Before they retired she curled up in her chair
and meditated, while Quintus smoked his cigar. All of a sudden she looked up and surprised him with this question, uttered in a
tone of vexed impatience :

"Why do people marry, Quint?"

"Well, my dear," he answered, slowly, puffing a ring of smoke toward the ceiling, "I
suppose it is because they would be lonely if
they lived apart."

"But you and I are not lonely, and yet we
are not married."

"That is because you and I are so fond of
each other that we don't want to run away
from each other, even if we are not married,"
he answered, laughing.

"Then marriage," she went on, with an air
of grappling earnestly with the question, "is
invented to keep people together who would
like to run away from each other."

"Not exactly that, darling," he said, becoming suddenly serious, "although that is unde-
niably an office which marriage is frequently
made to perform."

" Well, what is it meant for, then, Quint ? "

" It is intended to bind people more closely together who love each other dearly."

"Then why don't you and I marry, Quint? We love each other dearly."

She had come close up to him, and put her arms coaxingly about his neck, as if she were begging him for a new dress or bonnet.

" That is a thing which you don't understand yet, my sweet child," he replied, a little tremulously (for somehow the question, uttered so innocently, touched him deeply); " but you will know some day, when you are older."

" Yes, I do know, too," she cried, with sudden vehemence. " It is because you love Miss Dimpleton more than you do me."

And, bursting into tears, she rushed out of the room.

The scales had at last fallen from Quintus's eyes. He now wondered that he had been so persistently blind. Tita was jealous of Miss Dimpleton, not because she knew what love was, but from a childish, unreasoning impulse, as any pet animal is jealous if another threatens to usurp its place. The situation was getting more complicated than, in his Norse simplicity, Quintus had ever anticipated.

VII.

THE next day—it was a gray and frosty morning in February—a very unusual thing happened. Tita did not make her appearance at breakfast, and replied, to Quintus's anxious inquiries at her door, that she had a headache. When he returned in the evening, she had apparently recovered from her indisposition; but some strange, new spirit had taken possession of her, and he had to rub his eyes to be sure that he was not mistaken as to her identity. She received him, not with her old impulsive caresses, but with a stately grace, which was in keeping with yesterday's train, but not with to-day's shorter skirts. She presided at table with a dignity which was superb, and to his wondering gazes she responded with politely questioning smiles, as if she did not quite comprehend the reason for his astonishment. Quintus was sincerely puzzled, and would have felt justified in being angry, if Tita had not looked so ravishing just then in her offended dignity, with her beautiful, rebellious curls making a golden frame about her sweet, dimpled face. Dignity in a countenance of this type, though to the possessor it is undoubtedly very impressive, has rarely been known to alarm outsiders. Tita, however, was ignorant of this fact of natural history, and therefore persisted until bedtime in her majestic demeanor, while Quintus smoked in brooding discontent. For there were other things than Tita's caprices which troubled him. The next day would be Thursday, and he would be obliged to meet Miss Dimpleton, and probably to offer her an explanation. Then the foolishly guarded secret would at last be revealed, and very likely, when Tita was brought out, Miss Dimpleton would prove herself a kind and valuable friend to her. And with this consoling reflection he hung his meerschaum (a hollow and frightfully inflated Turk whom Tita had named the Eastern Question) in its proper corner on the wall, and, finding mademoiselle's chair empty, retired to bed. But

he scarcely divined what the morrow had in
store for him. And yet the sun had a singularly ominous look as it shone, small and remote, through the river fog on the following
morning. On reaching the office, Quintus met
Hanson coming out from his chief's private
room. It was rather unusual for Mr. Dimpleton to arrive so early, and still more unusual
for him to have private interviews with Hanson. However, life was at best a humdrum
affair, and would be still more so if a man were
not at liberty to do things which his neighbors
might regard as eccentric. With this and
similar sophistries, Quintus strove to soothe
his troubled spirits, while with absent-minded
haste he tore open the envelopes of his business correspondence, and with sudden and unaccountable pauses, as if he had lost the
thread of his thought, gave directions to the
clerks who came to receive his orders. A few
moments after Hanson's departure, Mr. Dimpleton, without taking the slightest notice of
Bodill as he passed, called for his carriage and
drove away, and, about two hours later, a

messenger boy handed him a note from Miss Jessie, in which she announced, in the most coldly formal manner, that she would be obliged henceforth to discontinue her Homeric studies, and that she would accordingly make no further demand upon his valuable time. About three o'clock in the afternoon, the head of the firm returned and sent a clerk to Quintus's desk, requesting that Mr. Bodill would favor him with a moment's interview. The door of the private office was carefully locked when he had entered, and Mr. Dimpleton, with an icy solemnity which seemed to make a perceptible change in the temperature of the room, motioned him to a chair and seated himself on the lounge opposite.

" I offered you a partnership in this firm, Mr. Bodill," he began, abruptly, " under the impression that you were a man of excellent habits and character—a Christian man and a man of honor. This firm, sir, has always prided itself on the blameless Christian character of its members. Now, I am well aware that, from the Old-World point of view, the

5

offence of which you have been guilty is a
venial one, and would there probably not interfere seriously with your social standing——"

"And perhaps, sir," interrupted Quintus,
springing to his feet, while his face burned
with indignation, "you will have the kindness
to inform me of what offence I have been
guilty?"

"I had a higher respect for you than that,
Mr. Bodill," retorted Mr. Dimpleton, in a
slightly impatient tone, as if to say that it was
of no use to contest his facts, which were beyond dispute. "Then you plead ignorance of
your guilt, do you? Well, sir, to a gentleman
of your principles, very likely, it does not as-
sume the character of guilt. But since you insist upon it, I have no objection to informing
you that I refer to the fact that, although un-
married, you have a daughter, as I am told,
nearly sixteen years old. And knowing well
how my family and I would look upon this
circumstance, you have carefully guarded your
tongue, and never in our presence made the
faintest allusion to her existence."

" And who told you, sir, that I have a daughter ? " inquired Quintus, now no longer in anger, but with calm disdain.

" It is of no consequence who told me. However, if it can gratify you to know, it was a man who has every means of knowing your life, both previous to your arrival in this country and after. I need not say that I refer to Mr. Hanson."

" And did Mr. Hanson tell you that Tita was my daughter ? " cried Quintus, opening his eyes wide in astonishment.

" He said he had not the slightest doubt that she was your daughter, and that you had been compelled to leave home. Your father, he said, is very irascible,—but it is needless to recount what you know so well. Moreover, he added a great deal of corroborative evidence, which would make it useless for you to deny."

" In that case, Mr. Dimpleton," responded Quintus, with the utmost dignity, " I suppose it would be agreeable to you—assuredly it would to me—if our business connection were dissolved, the sooner the better. If you can take the word of a former groom of my father's, who, moreover, offers you nothing but conjectures and impressions, and refuse even to hear my defence, then my respect for you suffers as severely as yours, according to your statement, has for me."

"I have anticipated this proposition," remarked the publisher, coolly, " and here is my check for the amount which is due to you as your share in the profits of the business."

Bodill, without even glancing at the check, put it in his pocket-book, and, bowing stiffly, took his leave. For several hours he sauntered aimlessly up one street and down another, rode, from sheer weariness, on the street cars to Central Park, and back again to the City Hall, dined absent-mindedly at a restaurant, and finally, before the accustomed hour for his return home had arrived, crossed the ferry to Jersey City. He feared to encounter Tita's questioning eyes, and sincerely hoped that her dignified mood of yesterday would prove something more than a fleeting caprice, as in that

case he might succeed in fortifying his heart
against compromising confessions. If Tita
was stately, he might be distant, and they
might avoid affectionate collisions, which would
inevitably lead, not to the revelation of the
truth, for that would have been impossible,
but to much enforced and ingenious deception,
which, to a conscientious man like Quintus,
was scarcely less unpleasant. He had hardly
entered his study, however, before he divined
that the latter alternative would be presented
to him. Tita, who was yet playing the Queen
Titania (as Quintus had humorously designated
her majestic rôle), no sooner discovered the
look of weariness and trouble which shim-
mered through the hypocritical cheerfulness
of his face than she forgot her studiously pre-
pared part, and, rushing forward, became once
more the old vehement, childish, and adorable
Tita.

" Quint, Quint," she cried, " what have they
been doing to you ? And to-night is your
Homeric evening, too. And yet you come
home so early. Has Miss Dimpleton been bad

to you, Quint? I never shall like her if she has."

"No, child," he answered, taking the lovely face between his hands and kissing it. "I am only a little tired, and would like a long, peaceful smoke."

"But you can't have it, Quint," persisted Tita, giving her head a decisive little shake, and looking, with her hair curling rebelliously over her forehead, like a determined little Shetland pony who is conscious that its perversity is not altogether unbecoming. "Something has gone wrong to-day, and you will have no peace until I know what it is."

But Quintus would only give her fables for facts, and she retired with the conviction that he had proposed to Miss Dimpleton and had been refused. But what a monster Miss Dimpleton must be to refuse Quintus! In her indignation at such iniquity, Tita even forgot to congratulate herself upon the removal of a dangerous rival. She felt too sad on Quintus's account to be glad on her own.

VIII.

DURING the remainder of February and all the month of March, Quintus kept up a hypocritical show of activity, always starting at the accustomed hour for the office, and spending the day in *cafés* and reading-rooms, and in aimless wanderings about the city. He once even fell asleep on one of the benches in the Union Square Park, and, on being awakened by a policeman, had much difficulty in persuading him that he was neither drunk nor a vagrant. Often he was seen trudging on through the dismal, chilly rain which New York rarely escapes during March, having apparently some serious purpose in view; but being utterly oblivious of the state of his clothes and the direction his feet were taking, he would sometimes find himself in the most dangerous and disreputable districts of the city. He attracted, however, no special attention. His tall hat looked shabby and weather-beaten, his coat was dripping wet,

71

and he was shivering from head to foot—the normal condition of the inhabitants of these neighborhoods. He would have much preferred to remain at home, seated in his easy-chair in his comfortable library; but in that case Tita would have drawn her inference, and an explanation would have been inevitable.

Tita, in the meanwhile, was not blind to the striking change in Quintus's appearance and temperament. She noticed with increased apprehension the daily deepening of the lines about his mouth and eyes, the listless stoop in his shoulders, and the look of extreme weariness in his whole countenance. She dared no longer coax and question him in her playful manner, for she suspected that the cause of his grief was too serious to be dismissed with a playful retort. Moreover, he showed a disposition to irritability, which, in so amiable a man as he, was quite alarming; and Tita, with the superior knowledge of her sixteen years, began to prescribe for him, as for a moral invalid, substituting cocoa for coffee at breakfast, and fruit for pastries at dessert, and making various other dietary changes, in which Quintus, without a suspicion of their cause, unmurmuringly acquiesced. Tita, however, failed to observe any beneficial effects from her remedies, and as Quintus continued to grow thinner and more hollow-cheeked she grew more and more anxious, and finally resolved upon a daring enterprise which she had long vaguely meditated. That Quintus was in love, there could be no reason to doubt. From the few novels she had read, she had learned that the symptoms of this ailment were very alarming and extraordinary. And further, as Quint knew no other ladies than herself and Miss Dimpleton, and whereas, if he were in love with herself, he would undoubtedly have told her so, there was no escape from the conclusion that he must be in love with Miss Dimpleton. Moreover, his melancholy had dated from the evening when the Homeric readings had ceased. What more probable, then, than that Miss Dimpleton had refused him that very night? Of course, after such an occurrence it would be embarrassing to continue the acquaintance. Thus reasoned the

sage little Tita. And although in an obscure
corner of her heart there had lurked a hope
that Quint would some day love her as dearly
as she loved him, she was resolved to be
heroic and to do all in her power to restore
his happiness. If Miss Dimpleton were aware
what a noble fellow Quint was, she surely
would not persist in her refusal to marry him.
But, of course, she could not know; she did
not know him as well as Tita did. Therefore
Tita concluded that it was her duty to go to
Miss Dimpleton and enlighten her. She would,
of course, have to choose a morning when
Quint, as she supposed, would be at the office.

In this adventurous mood, Tita donned her
walking costume and tripped demurely down
toward the ferry-boat. She took a street-car
uptown, and arrived without any mishap at the
door of one of those great, featureless masses
of brown stone in which the fashionable New
Yorker loves to dwell. She rang the bell, and
was promptly admitted by the colored briga-
dier in blue and yellow, who, as Tita presently
reflected, had been gotten up to match the fur-

niture. She sent up her card, upon which she had written, with much trepidation at her own daring, "Miss Hulbert," and in a few minutes Miss Dimpleton descended, held out her hand hesitatingly, and, with an interrogatory smile on her lips, said:

"Excuse me, but I do not remember having had the pleasure——"

"No, Miss Dimpleton," said Tita, as Miss Dimpleton showed no disposition to continue, "you have never met me before; but—but— please allow me to sit down and collect my thoughts a little, Miss Dimpleton."

She felt an alarming inclination to burst into tears; she was puzzled and frightened at the rashness of her undertaking. Miss Dimpleton seemed very formidable, too, with her clear gray eyes, and her smooth hair, and her rich and stately attire. She stood looking at poor Tita, as if she were deciphering her very soul.

"Yes, certainly, do sit down," she was saying, gazing with sudden intentness at Tita's card, which she was yet holding in her hand. "Your name, it appears, is Miss Hulbert. May

I ask, were you not the lady whom I saw with Mr. Bodill in the theatre about six or seven weeks ago?"

"Yes, probably I was."

"Then pardon me if I ask you embarrassing questions; but it is of some importance to me to know. Ought not your name to be Miss Bodill?"

"You mean that I ought to marry Quint?" exclaimed Tita, in hypocritical astonishment, while the tears trembled through her words. "Oh, not at all, I assure you. Of course, I love Quint very much, because he is so good and kind and lovely—oh, you don't know how good Quint is, Miss Dimpleton."

Somehow there was something very touching to her, just then, in Quint's goodness, and the tears refused to be held in check any longer, but coursed down her cheeks, while she yet bravely gazed into her rival's eye.

"I have no doubt Mr. Bodill is very good to *you*," replied Miss Dimpleton, a little stiffly, although she had to admit to herself that the impulsive and childlike manner of this young girl was very winning. Evidently Mr. Bodill had kept her in ignorance of his true relation to her, and under such circumstances it would hardly be kind to burden her with a knowledge which would necessarily give her pain. " But," she added, " pardon my frankness—but how does Mr. Bodill's goodness concern me ? "

"It concerns you very much indeed, Miss Dimpleton, if you only knew it," said Tita, resolved, however embarrassing it might be, to speak plainly. "Quint has been very ill of late, ever since the evening when you gave up your Homeric studies. I know that something must then have happened to him, although he has never told me what it was. Yet I know that it is you who must have done something to him that has wounded him very deeply. And, Miss Dimpleton, it was this I came to tell you, that if there ever was a man in this world who is thoroughly noble, from the crown of his head to the sole of his foot, that man is Quintus Bodill. It is a great pity that he should care so much for your company that it should make him ill and wretched not to see you. For, though you are very beautiful, you are not as beautiful as Quint; nor are you so good as he is, since you like to wound and grieve those who are fond of you."

Miss Dimpleton, instead of smiling at this intrepid arraignment, delivered in a tear-choked voice, grew suddenly very serious, and sat gazing with a look of earnest scrutiny into Tita's face.

" Listen to me, Miss Hulbert," she said, half unconsciously seizing Tita's hand. " You think I am cold and cruel, and that Mr. Bodill is a saint. Supposing it was I who was cruelly wounded, and that it was Mr. Bodill who had inflicted the wound. Unfortunately I cannot make you understand what I mean. But when a man creates an ideal of purity and nobleness in a woman's mind, and then carefully conceals the fact that he is himself far from worshipping at the altar which he erects for her; then —then "—Miss Dimpleton groped for a moment for the proper phrase—" there is no forgiveness for that man—and in all likelihood he would not even care to be forgiven. Suppose, too, that a woman had held aloof from society, and refused to squander her strength and blunt her sensibilities in fashionable dissipations; suppose she had hungered for a life of nobler aims and loftier interests, and fancied that this man held the key to the Eden she had dreamed of, and imagine then her indignation when she discovered that he, too, had soiled his hands in the moral filth in which the baser crowd of humanity grovel. Can you, with your sixteen years, imagine the bitterness which such an experience leaves behind it, and the dreariness and hopelessness which must follow ? "

Tita, who, without precisely understanding the nature of Miss Dimpleton's grievance, vaguely felt that Quintus's honor was being assailed, bristled all over with eagerness to rush to his defence. Her interlocutor, however, although she observed her impatience, was resolved to finish her indictment—not because she would condescend to demand sympathy, but merely to give vent to the righteous wrath and scorn which had accumulated within her. Now, at last, came Tita's chance to retort.

"Well, madam," she broke forth, forgetting entirely her benevolent purposes," if you mean to insinuate that Quintus Bodill is the kind of man you have just been describing,—I understand what you mean, and you needn't look pityingly at me,—then I can only say that— that you don't know him, and that you are unworthy of the honor of knowing him."

And, with a disdainful bow, Tita swept out of the room, whereupon the formidable blue-and-yellow negro opened the door. As she descended the steps, she met an elderly gentleman, who had just emerged from his *coupé*, and was running up the steps with an eagerness quite out of keeping with his years. She could not look him in the face for her tears ; but as she heard his latch-key in the door, Tita sagely concluded that it must be Mr. Dimpleton.

IX.

"TELL Miss Jessie I want to see her, as soon as possible," said Mr. Dimpleton to the servant.

"Miss Dimpleton is in the pa'lo', sah," was the reply.

The publisher, with a look of suppressed excitement, entered the room, and, without any preliminary, handed his daughter an opened letter. Miss Jessie, who was too absorbed with her own reflections to notice her father's manner, received the letter rather listlessly, and, supposing it to be an invitation, put it into her pocket.

"Why, my dear, I wish you to read it at once," said he; "it is a matter of great importance."

She sank into an easy-chair, unfolded the paper, and had hardly read ten words, when she started up again, and stared hard at her father.

" Where, where did this——" she cried.

" Read it, read it," he demanded, "and then tell me what we ought to do. Of course we owe him reparation."

The letter read as follows :

" Messrs. J. C. DIMPLETON & Co.

" GENTLEMEN:—We have been informed that you have in your employ a gentleman, about thirty-two years of age, named Quintus Bodill. A young man of that name crossed in one of our steamers about twelve years ago, and made himself the voluntary guardian of a little girl, then four years old, whose mother had died during the voyage. We made careful inquiries at the time, in the hope of discovering some friend or relative of the deceased, but all our efforts were in vain. As in all probability Mr. Bodill would have informed us of the child's death, and we have received no intelligence to that effect, we conclude that she must be alive, and yet under Mr. Bodill's protection.

" The occasion for our troubling you with this affair is the fact that a sum of $455 was collected among the passengers for the benefit of the orphaned girl, which sum was deposited with us, and invested in United States six per cent. bonds. Capital and interest are at Mr. Bodill's disposal whenever he will present himself, with proper identification, at our office. A messenger, whom we sent to your place of business to inquire for him, failed to find him, and we therefore beg of you to have the kindness to communicate to him the contents of this letter. We have the honor to remain, gentlemen,

"Very respectfully yours,

"BALLARD, RUSH & Co.,

"Agents for —— Transatlantic Steamship Co."

"If he had only not been so deucedly proud," said Mr. Dimpleton, in a dispirited sort of fashion—"if he had only deigned to offer me an explanation, all this trouble might have been avoided."

"How could he, father?" retorted Miss Jessie, passionately, letting the letter drop into her lap. "After what you said to him, there was but one thing for a man of honor to do, and that was exactly what he did."

"And who was it that prompted me to act so rashly as I did on such very slight premises?" asked he, with a remote approach to indignation.

"It was I, father, and I ought to suffer for it. But oh, if I had only known five minutes ago what I know now, I might, at all events, have avoided adding insult to injury! The young lady you met on the steps was the orphan referred to in this letter, and she came, evidently without his knowledge, to upbraid me, as I deserve to be upbraided, for my hasty condemnation, and for my whole ignoble conduct toward him."

Miss Jessie was in the contrite mood when there was a satisfaction in feeling the cut of the lash, and she would have bowed her head humbly under the application of the severest adjectives. And yet, through all this luxurious humility, there thrilled a sense of triumph at the thought that she had, after all, not bestowed her admiration, and perhaps something even more precious, upon one who was unworthy. She need no longer blush at her own want of insight and discrimination, and she need no longer writhe under the degradation of having opened the inner chambers of her soul to profane eyes. It will be seen that she was occupied chiefly with herself. She felt vaguely sorry for the suffering she had caused him, but her uppermost feeling was joy at being rehabilitated in her own sight. There was some satisfaction, however, in knowing that Bodill had taken her displeasure to heart, although, of course, she could not ascertain how much of his wretchedness was due to the loss of his position.

"Well, my dear," said her father, who was ever ready to do his daughter's bidding, "what do you propose to do now?"

"Order the carriage for me at four, please," she answered, after a moment's hesitation, "and we will both make Mr. Bodill a call and offer him our apologies. I believe he lives somewhere on the Jersey side?"

"Yes, we have his address at the office."

X.

TITA glanced with some uneasiness toward the door, and hastily secreted about a square foot of embroidery in a drawer, the key of which she put, with a triumphant little nod, into her pocket. She was making Quintus an elaborate Turkish smoking-cap, to go with his dressing-gown and slippers, so that, while indulging in the oriental luxury of smoking, he might be in character, as it were—entirely *à la Turque.* But it was, of course, of the utmost importance that Quint should have no suspicion of her deep design until April 5th, when he would be thirty-two years old. On his birthday she was, moreover, in the habit of making him presents of all the things which she conceived that he was in need of; and the bills were, of course, duly presented, one by one, with many days' interval, at times when he was incapable of being anything but amiable.

Hearing heavy footsteps, Tita imagined that it was Quint, who was returning from the office a little earlier than usual. Presently there was a knock at the door, accompanied by an ominous rustle of silk. Tita, with her heart in her throat, seized hold of the knob, and, without a thought of her toilet, turned it. It had never yet happened that any one had called upon her, and she naturally supposed that some one was making a mistake. When she beheld the stately forms of Miss Dimpleton and her father, she cast an anxious glance about the room (which, very likely, to feminine eyes, presented a disorderly appearance), then made a distant and dignified bow, and requested the visitors to be seated.

"The weather has been extremely capricious of late," remarked Mr. Dimpleton, gazing with a profound interest at the cornice of one of the tall book-cases which covered two walls of the room.

"Yes, I believe it has," said Tita, blushing to the edge of her hair, and feeling strangely agitated. She could not get rid of the impression that Mr. and Miss Dimpleton had come here on some errand of revenge, possibly to punish her for her insolence during the morning. In the next moment, however, she felt ashamed of these suspicions, and with an energetic effort set herself to the task of entertaining her guests. But unhappily she feared that she knew but little of social etiquette, and she had never felt so completely at sea with any one as with these two grave and apparently critical strangers.

"Mr. Bodill seems to be a good deal of a scholar," began Mr. Dimpleton again, just as Tita was meditating her first tentative remark.

"Yes, sir," she hastened to answer; "he takes great pleasure in his books, and he has some very rare ones, too. I am so sorry that he has not yet returned from the office, but he rarely returns until half-past five or six."

"The office?" repeated Mr. Dimpleton, in an interrogatory tone. "Is Mr. Bodill in business again?"

"He has never been out of business, as far as I know," retorted Tita; then, with a sudden clearance of vision, and anxiety in her voice, she added: "I supposed he was in business with you, sir. At all events, I never heard that he had separated from you."

"We—we are no longer together," replied Mr. Dimpleton, in a good deal of confusion. "We separated about six weeks ago."

"Six weeks ago!" exclaimed Tita; "and he has been going to the office every morning, and has returned every night at the usual hour."

"He has not been with me, I can assure you," asserted the publisher, severely. He was not finely enough organized to divine the motive for such a prolonged deception, and was inclined to judge Bodill by his own standard.

"Mr. Bodill evidently wished to spare you the pain of knowing that he was out of employment," said his daughter, whom Tita's mournful face had moved to compassion. Tita was having the most horrible compunctions in regard to a blue parasol with a lizard carved on its ivory handle; she had bought it with Quint's permission, but she well remembered

the expression of his face when she told him
the price.

Miss Dimpleton, too, by the way, had been
indulging a remorseful reverie, and had, like
Tita, arrived at the most uncomplimentary
conclusions regarding herself. This plainly
furnished room, with the long, serious rows of
books along the walls, and the great, well-worn
dictionaries on the revolving shelves at the
writing-desk, was an eloquent commentary on
the life of the man whom she had misjudged.
She felt here the spirit of the man, and she felt
that it was a noble spirit. Her own splendid
upholstery, upon which she had spent so much
time and study, was, for the moment, almost
repugnant to her, and she would willingly (on
a certain condition) have exchanged her luxury
and ease for the moderate prosperity and
scholarly interests to which these books and
engravings bore witness. Mr. Bodill's tender
regard for the feelings of his ward (not to
speak of Tita's extravagant eulogies) also gave
her a new clue to his character, and as the
picture grew toward completeness at every

fresh touch which her memory furnished, her own conduct appeared to grow blacker in proportion as his grew more noble.

While the two ladies were thus tormenting themselves, and while Mr. Dimpleton was examining Webster's Unabridged, which was lying open on the writing-desk, with an air of curious interest, as if it were the latest literary novelty, footsteps were heard in the hall, and Bodill entered. He looked worn and weary; the lines of his face indicated suffering; and the loving eyes of Tita read at once in these lines the painful history of his generous deception. The twilight, however, had imperceptibly been creeping into the room, so that Miss Dimpleton, who was less skilled in this kind of psychological divination, saw nothing but a tall, handsome man, who seemed to be very tired.

"Mr. Bodill," she said, rising and advancing to meet him, "we have come——"

"Miss Dimpleton!" he exclaimed, starting back in surprise.

"Yes, it is I, Mr. Bodill," she answered, in

her clear, calm voice. "My father and I have come to beg your forgiveness for a grievous wrong we have done you."

"Yes. The fact is, Mr. Bodill," interposed Mr. Dimpleton, in a hurried and embarrassed way,—"the fact is, it was a sad mistake—a very sad mistake, sir."

"It was more than that," insisted the daughter; "it was a cruel injustice and a grievous wrong."

Quintus, instead of answering, glanced with anxious tenderness toward Tita, who stood with mouth, eyes, and ears intent upon discoveries.

"Couldn't you please go down, Pussy dear, and tell Mrs. Hanson to postpone our supper until half-past?" he said, with visible uneasiness. "Tell her we have visitors."

When Tita, with a look of intelligent sympathy, and yet with evident reluctance, had left the room, he said :

"Now, Miss Dimpleton, I am at your and your father's disposal. Do, pray, be seated. The subject to which you refer is to me a very painful one, and, as it appears to me, it is of no use to tear open a healing wound."

"We have very weighty reasons for doing what we do," said Miss Dimpleton. "We owe it to ourselves as well as to you. I need hardly say that my father has come to offer you the only reparation which you can accept and he offer with justice to himself and to you. He begs you, as a favor, to resume your former relations with the firm."

"Yes, Mr. Bodill, we are anxious to have you resume your former relations with us," echoed Mr. Dimpleton, whose conversation in his daughter's presence was but a slightly modified version of her remarks. "We can do nothing less, in justice to ourselves and to you. I hope, sir, that that will be satisfactory to you."

"It is not a favor we offer," explained the young lady, with much earnestness, as Quintus sat leaning his head on his hand in meditative silence; "it is a favor we beg you to confer."

"It is very kind of you to put it in that way," answered Bodill, without looking up.

"Nevertheless, I cannot quite dismiss the thought that, if Mr. Dimpleton had valued me highly as a member of the firm, he would not have accepted my resignation so promptly, and listened so readily to rumors affecting my character."

"You force me to be explicit," replied she, with a little touch of excitement. "I shall be obliged to tell you, then, that it was not my father, but it was I, who accepted your resignation—that it was I who, if you choose, expelled you from the firm. My father had, and has, the highest appreciation of your ability, and has sincerely regretted your loss, and is now only anxious to have you accept our apologies."

It evidently did not occur to her that she was humiliating her father by this frank avowal, nor did it appear to embarrass Mr. Dimpleton in the least to have his daughter thus openly declare his dependence upon her. That she should rule and he obey, was part of the inscrutable order of things, which could not be remedied without a domestic revolution.

And as his yoke had been very gradually assumed, and had never been very hard to bear,
the revolutionary spirit had long ago died out
of him. On Quintus, however, Miss Dimpleton's frankness made an unpleasant impression; and although he could not conquer his
admiration of her beauty and her clear intellect, he began from this moment to discern
the alloy of baser metal in her character. And
it is marvellous how quickly the first questioning of a friend's motive, the first hint of censure, is followed by a host of critical suggestions, which in a short time, entirely transform
our friend's character. Thus, in Bodill's case,
the illusion was broken, and Miss Dimpleton
swiftly descended from the ideal heavens
whither she had flown with the strong wing-
beats of Homer's verse, and became an ordinary mortal—though, as such, a very beautiful
and interesting one.

While thoughts like these had been, more
or less consciously, occupying Bodill's brain,
Miss Dimpleton had risen, and her face had
assumed that vaguely abstracted air which, in a

lady visitor, indicates that she is on the watch
for a favorable opportunity to take her leave.
Her sire, to whom Bodill's silence was perhaps
a little vexatious, was once more absorbed in
Webster. He could not comprehend why a
young fellow should not jump at the chance of
becoming once more a partner in a business so
remunerative and so securely founded as his.
The daughter, too, who had anticipated no
difficulties in the path of reconciliation, was
beginning to feel a little impatient with his
scruples; but, being intent upon her purpose,
determined to make one more attempt.

"I had one other errand in coming here,"
she said, meeting Quintus's eye with her candid gaze. "I have taken a great fancy to your
ward, Miss Hulbert, and I beg you to lend her
to me for one year. I wish to bring her out in
society, and to complete her social education,
as far as you and she will allow me. I promise
you I shall not spoil her, and, if you wish it, I
will return her to you at the end of the year,
as pure and sweet and beautiful as she is now.
But, as you are undoubtedly aware, a man is

not the best educator for a young girl of her age; she needs some attentions that only a woman can bestow. Now, what do you say? I know the precious value of what I ask, and I shall treasure it as a faithful steward."

The praise of Tita, and the delicate retraction of all charges against him indicated by this request, touched the Norseman deeply. And yet, though he had long plotted a brilliant social career for Tita, he felt as if his heart was being wrung at the thought of losing her.

"I thank you—I thank you sincerely," he stammered, quite overcome with emotion; "but do not press me to-night. I do not refuse your offer, but I need time for reflection. To-morrow, if you will permit me, I will call upon you, and reply to both your kind propositions."

"And remember, please," said Miss Dimpleton, as she shook his hand at the head of the stairs, "that my admiration of your ward is no passing fancy. You know this is the third time I have seen her."

7

"The third time?"

"Yes. The first time was at Booth's Theatre. The second time was this morning, when she made me a call, which you see I have been very prompt in returning."

XI.

WHAT to do without Tita—that was a serious
problem. And yet—thus reasoned the wise
and conscientious Quint—what to do with Tita
might in time become a still more serious one.
She was growing up into womanhood, and all
her affections had centred on him, only because they had had no one else upon whom they
could centre. Was it fair, then, and generous
to keep her thus perpetually in ignorance of
the world? No; he would give her full liberty
of choice (he had an idea that Tita merely
needed to look at a man to have him fall a victim at her feet), he would allow her to enjoy
the triumphs to which her mind and her
beauty entitled her; and if, then, after a moderate experience of the world, she returned, with
an unwavering heart, to him—so much the
better; he would not possess himself of the
love of a woman surreptitiously, nor would
99

he bestow even wealth and happiness upon
her except by her own free and enlightened
choice.

Being, in the meanwhile, convinced of the
sincerity of the Dimpletons, and their mortifi-
cation at the injustice they had done him, he
also determined to accept their offer to reënter
the firm. He would thus be able to give her
the social advantages, such as they might be,
of a winter in New York. It was evident
Quint had a weak spot in his otherwise sound
composition. He desired for Tita distinctions
of whose worthlessness he was himself fully
convinced. He reasoned that it would be
cruel to have his prejudices in any way interfere with her pleasures.

It was a considerable surprise to him when he
found that Tita was not a party to his speculations—that, in fact, she was violently opposed
to all his ambitious projects. She had grown
up among his book-cases, and she was determined to remain there. If he was going to
marry Miss Dimpleton and become Mr. Dimpleton (Tita thought this a dexterous thrust),

why, then, of course she would have to give
her consent and, in the end, condone the offence by continuing to reside under their roof;
but her blessing she would withhold, unless it
proved entirely indispensable to their happiness. When Tita was in her bantering mood,
Quintus always sat beaming with paternal admiration, and thus frequently forgot his argument. And the little rogue, who was well acquainted with her protector's weaknesses, had
no scruples in employing this method of escape from disagreeable topics. The evil day,
however, was merely postponed. Quintus was
really this time in earnest, and Tita divined
from his persistence in argument that his mind
was made up, and that her dilatory tactics
were of no avail. She then yielded a graceful
acquiescence, and, without further remonstrance, allowed herself to be transferred to
the residence on Madison Avenue. It was on
the day of separation, when they were seated
together in the carriage, that he came near
asking her the object of her former visit to
Miss Dimpleton, to which he had never be-

fore alluded; but, being a great master in the mental arithmetic of affection, he was subject to sudden revelations, and, in this instance, at least, he knew that he had no need of asking.

XII.

Two months after Tita's arrival the Dimpletons broke up for the summer and went to Newport, where they owned a villa. Tita, of course, was removed with the rest of the baggage; and Miss Dimpleton, who counted much on the pleasure of bringing out a new and striking-looking young lady, had naturally taken pains to provide her with a sufficient number of effective costumes. All the dresses which had been manufactured by Mrs. Hanson, with the aid of the "Bazar," and even those which were the work of "fashionable dressmakers" who dealt in "*Modes de Paris*," were ruthlessly cashiered; in their places marvellous compositions of laces and flowers and satins were devised by persons who had seriously studied the art of hiding defects and emphasizing beauties, and harmoniously arranging all the multifarious details of a young lady's appearance. It was singular enough that the

Homeric Miss Dimpleton, who never aimed at
elaborate effects in her own toilet, should have
expended so much time and thought on triv-
ialities in her guest's behalf. She had, however, a dimly defined purpose, which, though
unacknowledged at first, gradually began to be
countenanced, and at last governed all her
actions. It had risen for the first time, consciously, in her mind when she made Bodill
the proposal to attend to Tita's social education ; but she had been ashamed of it, and had
persuaded herself that she had much more
laudable motives in assuming this responsible
charge. Crudely stated, she recognized in
Tita a rival, and she wished to make her harmless. And the simplest way to accomplish
this would be to marry her to another man.
She did not doubt that such an arrangement
would conduce to Tita's happiness as well as
to her own; at any rate, Tita must take her
chances in the matrimonial lottery as other
women did, and not foolishly aspire to an exceptional and ideal happiness, which was only
reserved for very exceptional persons like her-

self. Of course, that was not the way she formulated her argument, but it was nevertheless
the inevitable inference from her mode of reasoning.

Since her discovery of her mistake in regard
to Tita's birth, and especially since her visit
in his library, Bodill had become a moral hero
to Miss Dimpleton. She was not madly and
romantically in love with him, but she regarded him as a highly developed and exceptional specimen of the human race, and as
peculiarly fitted for a life-long companionship
with herself. He was supremely desirable to
her in every legitimate relation in which a man
could come to a woman, and she could see
nothing undignified or unwomanly in her exert-
ing herself to become equally desirable to him.
If a little extra manœuvring was needed, she
excused herself with the reflection that men
were naturally a little obtuse and less clear-
sighted than women, and would be more likely
to yield to an impulse of tenderness or of pity
rather than weigh rationally their chances of
happiness with two differently endowed women.

Tita more than justified Miss Dimpleton's
expectations in regard to her social success.
She made a sensation the first morning she
appeared on the beach. Within a short time
she "became the rage," to use the favorite
phrase of her admirers. Her toilets were
studied by hundreds of envious eyes, and re-
ported by the local correspondents of the New
York papers. Wherever Tita went (always
under Miss Dimpleton's protecting wing), gentlemen sprang up about her as if by magic.
During an hour in the morning, she held court
from her phaeton on the beach, and astonished
her protectress by the ease with which she
adapted herself to the conversational tone of
every one who came up to address her. In
the afternoons, when, during the fashionable
hour, she lolled at Miss Dimpleton's side in
their carriage, and returned, with a queenly air,
the salutations of the passing equestrians,
there was probably not a person the whole
length of the avenue who called forth more
exclamations of wonder and admiration, or
concerning whom more inquiries were made.

Miss Dimpleton congratulated herself on Tita's
receptivity for frivolous impressions, and reflected, with half-suppressed satisfaction, that,
without much effort on her part, the charming
little recluse of Jersey City was being trans-
formed into an accomplished worldling. She
had evidently needed only the opportunity.
Miss Jessie did not know, however, what a
superior and wholly philosophical view this
absurd little Tita was taking of the dazzling
Vanity Fair at which she was expected to
" assist " in a more active capacity than that
of a spectator. Nor was she aware that Tita
spent an hour every night, no matter how late
she returned home, in describing to Quintus
the doings of the day. Her daily bulletins
were, to the unprejudiced eyes of their recipient, the wittiest and most brilliant specimens
of epistolary writing that had appeared in any
literature. He read them aloud to Mr. and Mrs.
Hanson, who somehow failed to appreciate any
of the good points, and was even tempted to
take Mr. Dimpleton into his confidence, merely
to show him what a wonderful creature Tita

was. Many and many a lonely hour did he
beguile in reading and re-reading the funny
little backhanded epistles (for Tita's penman-
ship was her weak point, though her spelling
was irreproachable), gloating over the multitude of affectionate absurdities which were pre-
fixed to his name, and rejoicing in the fresh
and pure spirit which seemed to exhale from
every word and syllable. Of course he missed
her sorely, but the generosity of his love did
not allow him to pine, and far less to urge her
return. She was having a useful experience
of life ; and he—well, he was passing through a
necessary discipline.

Among Tita's many adorers, all of whom
were encouraged by the diplomatic Miss Dimpleton, there were especially two whose attentions toward the middle of the season grew
sufficiently pronounced to cause the usual rumors of engagements and refusals and recon-
ciliations, and whatever other contingencies
may occur in a man's pre-matrimonial career.
The one was Count von Markenstein, a former
attaché of the German legation at Washington,

and the other Mr. Horace Dibble, a very harmless young gentleman who had had the misfortune to inherit a million. The Count was a tall and superbly built man of thirty, with a beautiful blond beard, and hands which would have been no less remarkable if he had taken less pains to exhibit them to advantage. He was indefatigable in arranging sailing parties, to which he invited thirty ladies for the sake of concealing his preference for one; he trotted and cantered at all hours past the Dimpleton villa, with a view to showing his elegant horsemanship; and he bore with unfailing good-humor Tita's caprices, and her often very pointed rebuffs. Young ladies must be expected to be enigmatical, he reasoned, and they should be allowed a certain latitude in their caprices previous to marriage. But he was acquainted with a course of post-matrimonial discipline which would soon correct all little irregularities of conduct, sentiments, and opinions. The Count was an officer in the German army, and had great faith in the efficacy of discipline. Tita was far too fearless and independent, he thought; but as she was otherwise so wholly adorable, her minor failings might readily be forgiven until the time came for correcting them.

Poor Tita had not the remotest suspicion of the sinister designs which Count von Marken-stein was harboring in his bosom. To her he was merely a ponderous young man who waltzed delightfully, spoke indifferent English, and was inclined to be didactic. It was therefore a genuine surprise to her when, one evening, without a word of warning, he flung himself at her feet in the old operatic style, and made some preposterous requests which she never could think of granting. She fled in dismay into the library, where Miss Dimpleton was sitting deeply absorbed in Buckle's " History of Civilization," and declared that she was afraid the Count was ill. Miss Dimpleton, who supposed he had fainted, rushed into the par-lor with a bottle of *eau de Cologne* in one hand, and a decanter of water in the other, but saw nothing at all ludicrous in the situation when she discovered her mistake.

When Miss Jessie returned, Tita observed that she had that strained expression about her mouth which always indicated that she was angry.

"Tita," she said, in a severe tone, "I am greatly shocked to think that you could behave so rudely to a man of Count von Markenstein's importance. Why, any girl in Newport would be proud to receive his addresses."

"Then the Count has been making you a confession," said the undaunted Tita.

"The Count told me enough to give me the clue to the situation. And I was obliged to apologize for you."

"I am very sorry you took that trouble, for it was the Count who ought to have apologized to me for behaving so ridiculously. Now, tell me what would you have done if a man, whom you supposed to be sane, suddenly flung himself at your feet, and proceeded to recite what appeared to be a piece from 'Robert le Diable,' or some other lurid opera?"

"I would have raised him up, and told him

that we could converse to better advantage
standing or sitting."

"Well, that might have been better, I admit. And I will do that, next time a man
loses his reason in my presence."

"Perhaps this may have been your last opportunity," observed Miss Dimpleton, primly.

"So much the better. I always find men
more agreeable before they have taken leave
of their senses."

"And they would undoubtedly find you
more agreeable if you would control that
unruly tongue of yours, which wags very
thoughtlessly, and often makes witty but ill-
advised remarks. Men, my child, are not attracted by young ladies who have an eye for
their weaknesses, and who are capable of taking a humorous view of them."

"And tell me why should I be so anxious
to attract men? I never cared a straw for any
man but Quint ; and he always laughs at my
funny remarks, and kisses me, and says,
'Naughty Queen Titania!' and then I always
feel encouraged to go on."

"Mr. Bodill, I am afraid, has systematically spoiled you. He ought to have extracted the sting in your tongue while it was yet small, and not allowed it to grow until it is capable of doing you harm. You know that it is only the unmarriageable bees that sting, and they have to spend their lives working for the married queen and her children. But the married gentlemen bees, who failed to detect their charms, they despatch into eternity by way of revenge."

"What an admirable arrangement! I approve of that highly, although I should be sorry to see Quint fall a victim to a vindictive spinster when he finally makes his choice. I shall put him on his guard, however, and tell him to be sure not to fail to discover anybody's charms."

Miss Dimpleton looked up seriously from Buckle, whom she had all the while made a pretence of reading, and scrutinized Tita's face with an uneasy glance. But Tita looked so gay and innocent, it was impossible to believe her guilty of a malicious intention.

8

XIII.

ABOUT the first of October, the Dimpletons returned to the city. Mr. Dibble and the indefatigable Count also began to find the seashore unpleasant about the same date, and might have been seen at any time of the day, during the month of October, lounging at the windows or in the billiard-room of a certain club for fashionable idlers.

It was rumored that the Dimpletons were going to give a magnificent party for Tita, in order, as it were, to introduce her publicly as a recognized member of their social world and a proper recipient of invitations. Her success at Newport had made her a conspicuous personage, and there was much conjecture afloat regarding her origin. Whence she came and who she was, no one could tell with certainty; and Miss Dimpleton, whenever she was directly appealed to, always answered, placidly: "She is a dear friend of ours, whom we expect to spend the winter with us."

114

That was hardly sufficient to check curiosity; but as no further information could be elicited, and as Tita, moreover, was a young lady of fine bearing and social accomplishments, their circle of society in the city (as at Newport) was only too glad to accept her for what she was, without reference to her antecedents.

Miss Dimpleton, who had been much chagrined by Tita's supercilious treatment of her most eligible adorers, had resolved to manœuvre more actively in her behalf than she had ventured to do during the summer. She exerted herself earnestly to gain Tita's friendship and confidence, embraced her (a little awkwardly, perhaps,) at bedtime, and showed an affectionate solicitude for her comfort, which puzzled Tita the more because she could not more than half reciprocate. To her Miss Dimpleton always remained a formidable phenomenon. She told herself a hundred times a day that Miss Dimpleton was as kind as she could be; and whenever a disloyal thought would knock for admission to her mind, she would make an effort to brush it away as one does a cobweb. But cobwebs have a way of entangling themselves in one's fingers the more one tries to get rid of them; and she was greatly tempted to unburden her heart to Quintus, who came regularly twice a week to see her, and then usually stayed to dine with the family. But some curious, dim apprehension always checked her tongue, and, at all events, the open-hearted and innocent Quint would never suspect any human being of double-dealing, and far less of a complicated intrigue. She wondered what had happened to her, or what transformation she had undergone, since she left Quint. Instead of flinging herself on his neck at their first meeting after her return, as she had anticipated doing, and as she still longed to do, she had greeted him with a formal dutiful caress, and then seated herself to converse with him as if he had been an accidental acquaintance. Quintus, too, somehow seemed ill at ease; he sat gazing at her with an anxious smile, asked her how she had enjoyed herself, whether she would like to go back, etc. But it was evident that he was quite overawed by the splendor of her toilet, the perfection of her manner, and the whole newness of her personality. Tita felt the awkwardness of the situation acutely, and would have given worlds to know what Quintus was thinking about her. Never had he seemed to her dearer than in this moment. That good and noble face, those honest blue eyes, and the kind smile which lighted up his features so wondrously—she could never be tired of gazing at them. She excused herself immediately after dinner that night; and when Miss Jessie came up, an hour later, she found her lying on the tiger-skin rug before the fireplace, and sobbing like a heart-broken child. On inquiring, Miss Dimpleton learned that she, Tita, was not at all nice ; that, in fact, she was horrid, and that no one liked her except a ridiculous foreign Count and another man who hadn't two coherent ideas in his head. Against this species of unreason Miss Jessie felt herself utterly helpless. Nevertheless, from a sense of duty, she sat down calmly to refute Tita's assertions, beginning with her imputation against Mr. Dibble's intellect. Tita, however, refused to be comforted.

Scenes like this became more frequent as the months progressed, especially after Miss Jessie and Quintus had decided to resume their Homeric readings; and when they talked at the dinner table about the Greek ideal, as expressed in Hector rather than in Achilles, and compared these gentlemen with Siegfried, in the "Nibelungen" lay, poor Tita felt as if they had entered into a conspiracy against her happiness, and her tiny brain sometimes seemed about to explode with indignation. That Quintus could be so heartless as to sit and talk for a whole hour about topics which he knew were beyond her reach, when he must be well aware that Miss Jessie had introduced them merely for the purpose of making him feel her superiority to Tita—that was the drop which made her cup of woe run over. And to see his face light up with responsive ardor whenever Miss Jessie made a happy remark—as frequently

she did,—it was more than mortal heart could
bear. It never occurred to her that it might
be Homer and not Miss Dimpleton who was
her rival. She was too offended and indignant
to make such nice discriminations, and she inflicted much unnecessary suffering upon herself by the rashness with which she jumped
at mortifying conclusions. Another source of
annoyance was Mr. Dibble's unwearied attentions. Apparently he was conducting a
carefully plotted campaign against Tita's
heart. One week he assaulted her with bon-
bons in exquisite boxes of ingenious shapes;
and when that had no effect, he caused a floral
shower to descend upon her at the most unexpected hours. Another week he beguiled her,
with Miss Dimpleton as chaperone, to ride with
him in the park, in a turn-out and with a span
of roans which would have appealed, in their
possessor's behalf, to a heart of stone. Horse-
back rides, too, were proposed; but Tita could
not be induced to make the venture, ostensibly
because she had no confidence in her eques-
trian skill. Mr. Dibble's splendid bays (accom-

panied by a groom in buckskin knee-breeches)
stood pawing the pavement in vain in front of
the Dimpleton mansion; while Tita, hidden
behind the curtain in her bedroom, stood
battling with temptation, one moment on the
point of surrendering to the charms of the
horses, and in the next yielding to her fear of
Quint's disapproval, if she encouraged a man
whom she knew it would be impossible for her
to marry.

The Count, too, continued his visits at the
house, and had long interviews with Miss Dimpleton, from which both departed with pro-
digiously solemn countenances. Tita was beginning to congratulate herself on her freedom
from further persecution, when certain ominous
events happened which could not but cause
apprehension. The Count sent her a superbly
bound and illuminated copy of Thomas à Kem-
pis's "Imitation of Christ" (a gift from his
mother at his confirmation), and added a
high-flown inscription of his own which made
Tita shiver. To her it seemed a piece of im-
pertinence to send such a valuable gift to a

comparatively strange lady; and she would
have promptly returned it if Miss Dimpleton
had not peremptorily interfered. A very fortunate occurrence, however, soon turned the
tide of affairs in an unforeseen direction. On a
Sunday in October, the Count had, according
to his custom, met Miss Dimpleton and Tita
at church, and the former had invited him to
accompany them home and stay to dinner.
As they were walking down the avenue, con-
versing of indifferent things, the Count suddenly stopped to gaze at a newly repaired
church, and exclaimed :

"Oh, vat a peautiful shpeetle !"

"Yes, it is certainly very handsome," replied
Miss Dimpleton, gravely.

But Tita,—the unhappy Tita,—although she
knew perfectly how rude she was, began to
shake internally, and the more she tried to rid
herself of the "peautiful shpeetle" the more
irresistibly comical it appeared to her, and
after several moments of ineffectual struggle,
she burst into an uncontrollable fit of laughter.
She was about to apologize for her rudeness

when the Count, who had ignored her amusement as long as possible, now stiffly raised his hat and said :

"Ladies, I have the honor to bid you goodday."

That was the end of Count von Markenstein's courtship, and Miss Dimpleton now concentrated all her hopes on Mr. Dibble, who was of the slow and faithful kind, and had not sufficient confidence in his own irresistibility to risk a premature proposal. It was exceedingly provoking to be obliged to strike a name like that of Count von Markenstein from the list of one's visitors ; but as there was now no help for it, it had to be borne with philosophy. Moreover, Miss Jessie was not the ordinary type of snob who runs after great names whose only distinction is their antiquity. She was, perhaps, rather an intellectual snob, who would have felt prouder of a call from Browning or Herbert Spencer than of one from the Prince of Wales. She would have liked to rebuke Tita severely for her rudeness to the Count ; but fearing that it would be impolitic, and

might send the sensitive girl flying back into
Quintus's arms, she restrained her indignation,
and merely remarked that she regretted the
unfortunate occurrence.

XIV.

Tita's party was fixed for the sixth of December. All day long during the preceding week the *coupé* was in requisition, and the stores were ransacked in search of the choicest products which the market could afford. Tita's costume was planned with a seriousness as if the fate of the nation depended upon the disposition of this ribbon, or that bit of lace. Months before, *artistes* of international reputation had been consulted, and had submitted their designs, which were again submitted to others for criticism. Miss Dimpleton descended from her Homeric altitudes of thought, and discussed millinery, not enthusiastically and vehemently, as the majority of women do, but weightily and soberly, and with a minute attention to details which she never had displayed in her own behalf. She wished to make Tita so completely intoxicated with her success that a return to Quint's narrow world and sober

124

concerns would seem an utter impossibility;
and, judging by the ardor with which Tita frequently, when she was in the mood for it, entered into social enjoyments, she could not be
far wrong in supposing that the relapse into
her former obscurity was no longer contemplated with unalloyed pleasure. To be Mrs.
Dibble, with a million or more, would certainly,
to any properly constructed young lady, appear
preferable, especially when Mr. Dibble was
inoffensive and pliable—a mere unobtrusive
appendage to his wealth. Miss Dimpleton was
proudly conscious of being herself superior to
this kind of allurements, but then she had the
wealth already, and what she needed to give
dignity to these sordidly accumulated posses-
sions was exceptional refinement and intellectual culture. She wished above all things to
be exceptional, and the possession of moderate
wealth was by no means a claim to distinction
in New York. Tita, however, could not be expected to appreciate or to cherish such complicated ambitions. She had only blindly desired what happened, for very different and

loftier reasons, to be equally desirable to Miss Dimpleton; and she must be influenced to see that such a desire, on her part, was preposterous.

It was an amusing spectacle to see Tita, on the evening of December 6th, standing in the middle of her room with her elbows uplifted, and surrounded by an admiring circle of dressmakers and servants. A French *modiste*, with pins in her mouth and a determined frown (not of wrath, but of energy) on her brow, was kneeling behind her, bestowing her attention on some obscure fastenings about the skirt of the dress, and a maid was frisking about with flowers, and hand-glasses, and crimping-irons, and what not, in her hands, and bursting every now and then into ecstatic exclamations at Tita's loveliness. Tita, whose vanity had been persistently fed during the last eight months, could almost feel herself grow taller as she contemplated the effect of this rich and marvellous attire in the pier-glass. She walked like a queen, and heard with delight the silken rustle of her train.

A little after nine o'clock, the guests began
to arrive. When the bell rang for the first
time, Tita's heart shot up into her throat. She
ran (or, rather she would have run, had her
dress permitted it) toward the parlor door
where Miss Jessie was standing, and took her
station at her side in the prescribed attitude.
She ran rapidly over all her instructions in her
head, and got her mouth into position to say
what she had been told was proper to say,
raised her eyes slowly, when, lo and behold—
Quint! That was too much for Tita's com-
posure. She was about to yield to her mirth
in her usual hearty fashion, when Miss Dimpleton, foreseeing accidents, said, grimly: "Remember your dress, please," and Tita immediately sobered. Quintus still stood bowing in
front of her, and wondered what there was in
his appearance that was so ridiculous.

"I wanted to be the first to see Queen Titania in her glory," he said, with a curious look,
which was both diffident and searching. "I
wanted to see her before the glare of the light
shall have paled her loveliness never so little,

and before the jostlings of the crowd shall have rubbed the flower dust off her butterfly wings."

"I suspect that metaphor is intended as a rebuke to me," said Miss Dimpleton, with a tentative smile. "It was I who undertook to guard Tita against such calamities."

"It was not my intention to reproach any one," said Quintus, as he pressed Miss Dimpleton's hand and turned to give place to the next arrival. Just then Tita caught a glimpse of his back, and suddenly observed that his dress-coat was very old-fashioned. The sleeves were too tight and the skirts too long, and the lapels smaller than the fashion of the day required. Should she allow him to go about in that costume, which certainly would make him conspicuous in a very undesirable manner, and render him ridiculous in the eyes of the people? No; she would rather take the risk of displeasing him. He, of course, would never detect what sort of figure he cut; but, during these months, she had grown to be acutely sensitive to the world's opinion of him.

"Quint," she said, touching his arm gently, "pardon me if I venture to be impertinent, but you know it is an old privilege of mine. Would you, as a favor to me, take a cab and drive down to a tailor on Broadway, whose address I will give you? He makes a business of hiring out dress-coats to gentlemen; and yours, dear Quint, is not exactly stylish."

"Why," exclaimed Quint, in astonishment, "it was made for my graduation, and I haven't worn it much since."

This seemed to Quint's unworldly intellect a striking proof that his coat must be strictly *comme il faut*. He had worn it on so important an occasion as his graduation, and in the presence of a select audience; and as he had rarely worn it since, it was evident that its stylishness had remained unimpaired.

"You know you don't understand those things, Quint," said Tita, with an appealing look. "And now I can't explain them to you. But, pray, do what I ask of you."

"Well, anything to please your majesty," he answered, with a puzzled smile, which to Tita

9

was quite pathetic. She followed him with her eyes as he mounted the stairs, and saw him look at the sleeves of his coat with an air as if to say :

"Well, I should like to know what it is that isn't right about you."

When he returned, an hour later, with an irreproachable coat, the large *salon* was crowded, and the red-and-white awning which led from the carriages to the front door was crowded with rustling and perfumed couples. Tita still stood at the door, bowing and handshaking, but her smile was perhaps a little forced, and her flushed cheeks seemed to indicate that something was laboring within her. The fact was that, since Quint's departure, she did not feel at all so sure that she had done right in criticising his remarkable dresscoat. The mere suggestion of a criticism on her part must have appeared like black ingratitude to him; and, moreover, there is always a hint of patronage or superiority in even the mildest comment on clothes and personal appearance. When she saw Quint trying to wedge his way unnoticed into the back parlor, she held up her fan, and after a moment's hesitation he came toward her.

"Have you forgiven me, Quint?" she asked, remorsefully, while she pressed his hand warmly. "You know it would make me very unhappy to think that I had displeased you."

"You did right, my dear," he answered, kindly, "to give me a hint which no one could have given me but you."

Mr. Dibble now came to claim Tita's partnership for a waltz which she had been rash enough to promise him; and excusing herself to Bodill, she presently swung out upon the floor, encircled by Mr. Dibble's arm. Quintus, who so often in spirit had anticipated his unselfish delight at witnessing just such a spectacle, felt a horrible pang darting through him, and would have liked to strangle Mr. Dibble for presuming to touch her. Hardly had the young millionaire conducted her to her seat, before a dozen other gentlemen surrounded her, and displayed an extraordinary eagerness to scrawl their names on her card. Quintus observed, with a certain contemptuous admiration, that their hair, their moustaches, and their clothes were in that state of absolute perfection which is unattainable in any one who does not make the study of his toilet an absorbing business. He discovered for the first time his own inferiority in point of sartorial and tonsorial finish, and, strive as he might, he did not quite succeed in feeling proud of it.

During the rest of the evening and half the night, Tita was in incessant demand. Men who imagined that manliness required them to take a cynical view of women stood in groups about the supper-table and raved about her. Even upstairs in the billiard-room, where a dozen disenchanted bachelors in the thirties and forties were lounging and discoursing social ethics over fragrant cigars, it was frankly admitted that the man who should catch her might be considered a lucky dog. A foreign ambassador, whose acquaintance the Dimpletons had made at Newport, and who was the great light of the evening, put the stamp of his approval upon Tita, and thereby made it "good form" to be enthusiastic about her. He declared that she was *ravissante,* and that she would be sure to make a sensation in the great *salons* of the Old World. He thereupon danced a dignified quadrille with her, and came near making her famous by kissing her hand at parting.

Quintus, who had been roaming from room to room like an uneasy ghost, could not help perceiving that Tita's party was a success, and that she herself was exciting universal admiration. This was exactly the situation he had dreamed of in his early aspirations for her—she fêted and worshipped, and he standing by blissfully enjoying her triumph—at all events, he endeavored to persuade himself that the latter half of his prophetic hope was as fully realized as the former. He attributed all his present discontent to the trifling episode of the dress-coat, which, he thought, had somehow untuned him for the evening. He would have entertained a perfect contempt for himself if he had been forced to recognize the fact that, so far from being that unselfish and fatherly individual which he had fondly imagined himself to be, he was, on the contrary, at the present moment in a rage of jealousy. Every one who touched Tita or whispered a flattering platitude in her ear became, that very instant, his natural enemy, and he began, in a dim and general fashion, to cherish murderous designs against him. These sleek, well-tailored young gentlemen with well-bred smiles and well-trained moustaches became positively odious to him, and he would have liked, on philanthropic grounds, to exterminate the whole species. What empty and meaningless lives they must lead! and what vapid thoughts must move within their well-trimmed craniums! Surely Tita was worthy of something better than this shallow and frivolous fate. Why did Miss Dimpleton, who had herself so many nobler interests, exert herself to make Tita value the things which she herself professed to despise? To be sure, he had himself given his consent to have her introduced to society, and as this was society, it was evident that he had no cause for complaint.

While making these lugubrious reflections, Bodill had been seated in a corner of the billiard-room, smoking and listening to the intermittent and fragmentary remarks of the players. When he had finished his cigar, his uneasy curiosity about Tita prompted him to descend once more to the first floor, whence a subdued hum of music rose, and burst into sudden distinctness whenever the door was opened He had just reached the first landing of the stairs when he was suddenly arrested by the sound of two voices talking earnestly together, and, looking down, he saw Tita and Mr. Dibble, engaged in a hushed but excited conversation.

"I tell you, it is impossible, Mr. Dibble," Tita was saying. "We are not at all suited for each other ; and then I don't love you at all ; so, of course, it is out of the question."

"But I love you enough to make up for it," persisted Mr. Dibble. "If you will only marry me, I am willing to take my chances afterward."

Quintus, who had made his shoes creak loudly at every step he took, now interrupted the interview and passed down the stairs. Tita looked up, a little startled, but seeing who it was, she jumped up and seized his arm with something of her old vehemence.

"Oh, Quint," she said, gazing affectionately up into his eyes, "how glad I am that I have. found you! Dear Quint, there is no one like you."

In her joy at having escaped from Mr. Dibble's embarrassing importunities, she felt an irrational impulse to embrace Quintus, as something dear and familiar amid all the perplexing novelties which surrounded her. In his felicity at having her near him, he quite forgot to answer, and before they reached the ground floor they were joined by Miss Dimpleton, who was making a visible effort to be amiable. Tita, to whom Quintus's silence appeared enigmatical, supposed that he intended to repel her and ascribed his changed conduct toward her to the increased frequency, of late, of the Homeric lucubrations. Therefore, with the impulsiveness which characterized all her actions, she let go his arm, made him a sweep-

ing bow, and accepted the escort of a downy-
bearded young gentleman, who, with a card in
his hand, stood expecting her. Quintus opened his eyes wide in astonishment, and then
looked questioningly at his hostess, as if he
hoped that she would offer him an explanation.

"What is the matter with the child?" he
asked, finally.

"Tita has grown very capricious of late,"
answered Miss Jessie. "The homage and incessant flatteries of her many admirers have
turned her head."

"Poor little girl!" said Bodill, compas-
sionately. "She has not learned yet how little
those things are worth."

"I have—endeavored to teach her," Miss
Dimpleton was about to say, but then she remembered that that was not strictly true, and
she dexterously turned the half-uttered phrase
and said :

"I have frequently regretted her suscepti-
bility to flattery."

To her surprise, Mr. Bodill, instead of looking shocked, gave a low laugh as he said :

"To think of little Tita being courted and wooed, distributing judicious snubs and listening to tender nonsense. It is very amusing."

Mr. Bodill certainly was a very puzzling character, thought Miss Jessie, and he thought so himself, too, as he remembered how, only a moment ago, he had been devoured with jealousy of Tita's adorers, and had been well-nigh ready to join their ranks himself. But the note of censure in Miss Dimpleton's voice had aroused all his old paternal tenderness, and made Tita again seem the child that needed his protection.

XV.

IT was toward three o'clock in the morning when the last indefatigable dancers ceased to whirl in a ring, when the ladies ceased to wind through the fascinating figures of the German, and the musicians ceased to perspire over their violoncello, harp, and violins. The striped awning, constructed for the protection of delicate toilets, proved very useful to the departing guests, who would otherwise have been drenched on their way to their carriages. For a south-west wind, accompanied with rain and sleet, had sprung up during the early part of the night, and was now whirling up the avenue, lashing the window-panes and pulling vigorously at the few exposed shutters.

Tita, quite exhausted with excitement and the incessant motion, had just retired to her room, where her maid was engaged in taking down and combing out her hair, when Miss

139

Dimpleton entered, having first announced her intention with a knock.

"Margaret," she said to the maid, "leave us for a few moments."

She seated herself with her usual deliberateness in a pink satin easy-chair (which seemed created for lotus-eating), pulled off her slippers (which were not created for walking), and as a preliminary, let her eyes wander about the luxuriously furnished apartment.

"Tita," she said at last, rubbing her feet over the delicious nap of the tiger rug, "tell me now, honestly, whether you have any intention of returning to your former mode of life."

Tita, who was apparently engaged in disentangling the hearts which, in the course of the night, had got caught in the golden meshes of her hair, looked up with a startled glance, and was for a moment at a loss for an answer.

"I have a very particular reason for asking," continued Miss Jessie. "I cannot look on with indifference when I see you coolly, and almost contemptuously, rejecting every chance

which presents itself of providing for your
future, and gaining an established position in
society."

"Mr. Dibble has been making a confidante of
you, I perceive," remarked Tita, with a hair-
pin in her mouth, and letting a great golden
wave roll down upon her bare shoulder.

"It matters little who has been making a
confidante of me," retorted the other, sharply.
"The question is, what you really mean by
such unaccountable behavior?"

"My year will soon be up," said Tita, in-
specting with much interest the ends of a yellow lock which apparently had some mysteri-
ous peculiarity, invisible to the uninitiated,
"and if you desire it, I am quite willing to
take my leave at short notice. But I will not
submit to dictation" (here the yellow lock was
dropped and forgotten) "from any one in regard to my choice of a husband, as that is a
question which really concerns no one but
myself and the unfortunate man who is rash
enough to take me."

"It was not my intention to dictate," an-

swered Miss Dimpleton; "and I think it is
very ungenerous in you to suspect me of such
a sordid motive as you have just implied. I
need hardly assure you that we shall be glad
to keep you here as long as you are willing to
stay. If I presumed to offer my advice in the
question you refer to, it was only because, in
such a matter, I distrust your judgment, and
that of any one of your age, and imagine that
my own knowledge of the world might be of
some use to you."

Poor soft-hearted Tita felt immediately remorseful. She had been ungenerous ; but it
was only because she was so horribly tired
that she could not think one rational, far less
a generous, thought. If Miss Jessie would only
forgive her, she would listen calmly and col-
lectedly to all the matrimonial suggestions she
might have to offer, although she would not
promise beforehand that she would act on all
of them.

"But husbands are such peculiar creatures,
you know," she said, trying to coax her com-
panion out of her severe mood. "I never could

imagine what I should do with one. I don't dislike Mr. Dibble now; but if I couldn't escape from his society at pleasure, I know I should not be able to endure him."

"Tita, you are incorrigible," said Miss Jessie, relaxing a little from her rigid gravity. "What is ever to become of you, if you persist in taking a humorous view of every man who approaches you?"

"But, to be honest, now, don't you think yourself that men are ridiculous, always, of course, excepting Quint?"

The question was asked with such evident sincerity that it certainly deserved a sincere answer; but Miss Jessie, for reasons sufficient to herself, could not very well express her cordial agreement with Tita's sentiments, and as she was strictly conscientious when a direct question of right and wrong was at issue, she resorted to her inconvenient habit of silence. Tita felt once more rebuffed, and resumed her occupation with her hair.

"What I came to ask you," began Miss Dimpleton, after having gazed for a while into the fire in the grate, "is whether your refusal of Mr. Dibble is really final? As you know, he is a man of great wealth and of irreproachable character. He would treat you well, supply lavishly all your wants, and undoubtedly make you as happy as women have any right to aspire to be."

Tita looked absently at the reflection of her beautiful self in the glass, then flung herself back in the chair and contemplated the frescoed Cupids in the ceiling.

"I am so tired, so very tired," she sighed. "Why do you insist upon tormenting me at this unearthly hour?"

"Then I am to understand that you have not made up your mind definitely?"

"No, you are not to understand that. I have made up my mind once for all. You look upon marriage from a different point of view from what I do. Quint says that marriage is intended to bind two people more closely together who love each other dearly. But I do not love Mr. Dibble, and I never shall love him."

"Mr. Bodill is an impractical enthusiast, whose advice in such a matter it would be very unsafe to follow."

Tita sprang up as if something had stung her. The least implication of disrespect to Quintus always roused her as nothing else.

"No," she cried, "Quint is not an impractical enthusiast; and his advice is always good and noble as he is himself."

On Miss Jessie this violent partisanship for Bodill had at this moment a very irritating effect. It proved to her that all her labor had been in vain. And was she, who had been accustomed nearly from her cradle to rule, who felt herself the intellectual equal of the first men in the city, was she to be thwarted in her carefully laid plans by the caprices of this insignificant doll of a girl? Her first line of tactics had failed, but she had another in reserve.

"Have you ever reflected, Tita," she said, after another long pause, "upon your position as an inmate of Mr. Bodill's house? You are no longer a child, but a grown-up woman, and as such you can hardly, for your own sake, con-

10

tinue to live on such familiar terms with a
young bachelor of thirty-one or two. He is
not your father nor your brother, and the world
will naturally ask, 'What is your relation to
him ?' And, for your own sake, as well as for
his, you must heed what the world says."

A sweetly perplexed look had settled upon
Tita's features as Miss Dimpleton commenced
this speech, but gradually she grew pale, and
suddenly grasped at the back of the chair for
support.

"I don't understand—what you mean," she
gasped, and in the next instant looked as if a
scarlet veil had been flung over her face.

"I mean," Miss Jessie went on, pitilessly,
"that your remaining with Mr. Bodill or returning to him is an impossibility. You may
not have been aware what an amount of trouble
you already have caused him. When he was
discharged, or, if you choose, was forced to re-
sign his position in my father's firm, it was on
your account. We had been told that you were
his daughter, and as he had informed me that
he was not married and never had been, my

father naturally took offence. The situation is now no better. In fact, it is worse. Who knows who you are? You do not know yourself who was your father, and still you royally reject one of the best matches in New York. You think——"

Miss Jessie had wrought herself into a frenzy of eloquence; she hardly meant to be as cruel as she was, but she was determined to bring out her last reserves and to use her heaviest artillery. But while she was yet in the midst of her tirade, something half a sob and half a stifled groan burst from Tita's bosom, and flinging her arms above her head, she rushed toward the door and was gone. Miss Dimpleton, eager to finish her arraignment, leaned back in her chair, expecting that she would presently return; but a minute or more passed, and a current of cold air swept up through the halls and shook the doors. The windows, too, rattled sympathetically, and the pictures moved on the wall. Just then the wind drove the rain against the large panes with a sound as of a handful of pebbles;

Miss Dimpleton shivered. More minutes passed; the bronze clock sounded four distinct, melodious strokes. Miss Dimpleton rose and rang for the maid.

"How cold it is," she said. "Is anything the matter with the furnace?"

"No," answered the maid, "but the front door was open. I just closed it."

Then the truth flashed upon her; she heard for a moment only the blood pulsing in her ears, and that vague oppression which follows the first consciousness of a calamity stole over her.

"Call father quickly," she said, as soon as she could catch her breath, "and order the horses."

XVI.

TITA had acted under an impulse too strong
to admit of reflection. She felt outraged and
insulted by the suspicion cast upon her birth,
and still more by the cruel insinuation which,
in her innocence, had never once occurred to
her. She had always been with Quintus, and
it was proper and natural that she should be
with no one but Quintus. Heedless of her attire, she had hastened down the stairs and out
through the door, desiring only to hide herself, to escape humiliation, to get as far away
as possible from Miss Dimpleton, who could
think such base thoughts and inflict deep
wounds so pitilessly. She had not even remembered the rain, nor had she thought
where she was going. It was not until she
was several blocks away, and the driving sleet
had benumbed the tender skin of her neck and
face, that she slackened her speed and began
to consider whither her feet were carrying her.

149

To go back to Quint—that was out of the question. Had she not been a perpetual burden to him from the hour when he first pressed her to his warm and faithful heart? But where could she go, if she did not go to Quintus? He was her only friend, her only comfort and refuge in all the wide world.

The wind boomed through the long solitary streets, and the little satin slippers were soon as wet as so much paper. Her costly garments swept over the muddy sidewalks, and having become thoroughly drenched, clogged her limbs in their flurried and precipitate motion. Her hair felt like a cold wet lump on her neck, and sent repeated shuddering chills through her frame. Her step, too, was becoming feebler, and though she bore up bravely, she knew that her strength would soon be exhausted. It was a dim consciousness of this which arrested her flight. She leaned against a lamp-post for support, and gazed up at the great dark front of a fine residence, where only a single room was lighted. She suddenly recognized the house—it was Mr. Dibble's. It

was only two weeks since she was there at a
luncheon party with Mr. and Mrs. Dimpleton.
As she stood there, numb and ready to faint
with weariness, the demon woke in Tita's
heart, and she could not but listen to the
thoughts which he whispered to her. Was
not comfort like this—soft, warm, and luxurious—worth all the abstractions of love, honor,
and duty? Who would blame her if, from
mere powerlessness to resist any longer, she
yielded to the importunities of her adorer, and
satisfied herself with the common sordid lot of
common sordid humanity? She was a very
small woman, and a colossal heroism could
hardly be expected of her. There was evidently nothing for her to do but to return to
Miss Dimpleton and meekly beg her pardon
for the commotion she had occasioned.

Out of the depths of darkness came the
sound of chimes, striking the quarter hour.
By some strange association of sound or
thought, this clear, mellow tone brought up
Quintus's face vividly before her; and a rush
of feeling, quite as indefinable, brought back

the sweet memories which that face suggested. She remembered what he had taught her, year after year, through the long winter nights, and she yearned with all her soul to throw herself upon his neck and weep repentant tears upon his bosom. The temptation to go back to her recent life was gone ; and turning her face resolutely away from the house, she gathered her strength and trudged on. Farther down the avenue she found an empty cab, and ordered the driver to take her at once to Jersey City.

About this time Miss Dimpleton and her father were also driving through the storm and the darkness, and, after a vain search, went to police head-quarters and gave notice of Tita's disappearance.

On his return home from the Dimpleton party, Quintus had found a fire drowsing in the fire-place in his study, and, thinking that it was a pity to have it waste its genial warmth, he had seated himself in his accustomed chair and taken down a volume of Emerson containing the essay on Fate. This Olympic meditation had never yet failed to inspire him with a sense of serene superiority to all the petty annoyances of life, which not even a transcendental philosopher can escape. From the upper ether of his Emersonian mood, where the large expanses of time and space spread out gloriously around him, he could view even his love for Tita as an affair of small moment, which would not perceptibly affect the destiny of the race, and which in a hundred years would presumably be forgotten. The agitation of the ball was still tingling in his nerves, detached bits of Strauss waltzes were humming in his brain, and the pang of jealousy was yet nestling, like a dull pain, somewhere about his heart-roots. But the mighty thoughts of the sage, like solemn organ-tones, marched through the sounding eternities, on either hand, and lifted him with their strong upward impulse. The small emotions were soothed into a troubled calm, and life seemed once more dignified and noble.

While Bodill was thus holding discourse with the universe, he seemed distinctly to hear some one calling his name ; but, as he was frequently subject to this illusion, and sometimes had started up to answer when no one was near, he only turned about in his chair and smiled at the vividness of his imagination.

" —— if limitation is power that shall be," he went on reading, " if calamities, oppositions, and weights are means and wings——"

But surely that was the sound of a voice in distress, and the voice was familiar. His blood ran cold with terror, as he rushed to the window and strove to raise it. His strength had almost deserted him. With a second effort, however, he succeeded. The blinding sleet beat against his face, and a gust of wind swept in and whirled the sparks and ashes of the fire about the room. Under the lamp-post he discerned dimly a woman, who was gazing up toward his window.

" Oh, Quint, Quint ! " she cried, " open the door quickly ! It is I—Tita."

Her voice broke in the last words with a pitiful hoarseness which cut him to the heart. In an instant he was down the stairs, had torn the front door open, and clasped the trembling form in his embrace. Her bare arms felt like ice as they clung about his neck, and the congealed sleet hung unmelted in her hair. She made no attempt to speak, but lay listless in his arms, as he bore her up the creaking stairs and entered the old, well-known study. But, as he placed her upon the lounge and pushed it up before the fire, she drew his head close down to her mouth, and whispered :

"I will never leave you again, Quint—never!"

"No, my darling," he answered, fervently, "never!"

XVII.

Tita lay ill for a long, long time, and her life was often despaired of. It was not until the spring was well advanced that the color began to return to her cheeks ; then the old merry sparkle was again kindled in her eyes, though at first feebly and pathetically flickering, and the old, hearty ring sometimes stole into her laughter. At the least such sign of reviving strength, Quint's face would beam as he sat drawing meditative little puffs from the glowing depths of the Eastern Question. It was one evening while they were thus seated together before the fire, she occupied with some feminine handiwork, and he reading aloud from Browning, that an incident of vital importance to both occurred. The poem which was engaging Quintus's attention, and which he stopped every now and then to discuss with Tita, was appropriately entitled " By the Fireside," and in it was a stanza which moved him deeply :

> " Oh, I must feel your brain prompt mine,
>   Your heart anticipate my heart,
> You must be just before, in fine,
>   See and make me see, for your part,
>   New depths of the Divine."

"Now, that is my idea of what a marriage should be," said Quint, putting the book face downward, on his knee.

"It is very beautiful," remarked Tita, without looking up.

"But there is only one heart," he went on, quite naturally, " which could anticipate mine, and one sweet face which is to me a daily revelation of the Divine."

"I can't imagine what face that can be," observed Tita, looking up with roguish, tear-filled eyes.

"But I can," cried Quint, taking the face in question between his palms, and gazing ardently at it. " Tita, dear, why should we hesitate to take the step which will prevent our ever being parted again ? "

Tita smiled. She could not see why.

THE MOUNTAIN'S FACE.

THE MOUNTAIN'S FACE.

I.

THE cataract hummed a strong, steady under-
tone, and the lighter summer sounds—the whir
of the locust and the warble of thrushes and
linnets—rose fitfully and vanished against the
heavy background like sun-flushed mists on a
dark sky. The river, which flowed white and
strong in the deep, sang strangely toward
night, and followed you like an unconscious
melody, wherever you went. But if you stopped to listen to its voice, the melody vanished
and you heard nothing but a vague, tumultuous
brawl. The wind, too, sang in the tree-tops;
and in the grass there was a soft, unceasing
whisper which was strangely alluring and
sweet. From everywhere sounds seemed to be
oozing forth gently, dancing in the daylight and

vanishing. The vault of the sky seemed a vast
ocean of sound.

"It is strange, father, isn't it?" murmured
Ingolf, looking toward his father with a face
singularly lighted up from within, and eager
for sympathy. He was a blonde-haired lad of
about sixteen, with large lustrous eyes, and a
timid or tentative smile playing about his lips.

"What is strange?" asked his father, gruffly.

"The melodies in the air—and—and in the
grass," answered the boy. His voice grew feebler and, as it were, apologetic as he spoke,
and he finished in a tremulous whisper. He
looked unhappy and seemed to regret having
spoken.

"I hear no melodies," said the father with a
vindictive emphasis, taking his clay pipe out of
his mouth, and spitting with angry energy.

The boy sighed and was silent. With un-
averted eyes he sat staring at the western
mountain chain, which rose like a huge wall
tracing its dark outline sharply against the
sky. The same strange illumination again
broke over his countenance, as if a lamp had

been lighted within, shimmering through the translucent surface. His father gazed at him with ill-concealed vexation, but gradually his wrath changed into sadness.

"What is it now, you miserable boy?" he exclaimed, shaking his head mournfully. "What are you hearing now?"

"It is the mountain's face," cried the boy joyously. "I have seen it ever since I was a small boy, but I have never spoken of it, because I was afraid you would be angry. But surely, father, you cannot help seeing it now. It is so large and beautiful."

The father strained his eyes and stared for some moments, earnestly, at the mountains which rose black and threatening against the glory of the sunset.

"There, there, father," ejaculated Ingolf, pointing excitedly toward the western sky. "Just follow the direction of my finger! There you see the beautiful brow; it is that of a woman reclining. Sometimes she seems to be dead; sometimes only lightly asleep. To-night she sleeps with her hands folded upon her

breast; then follow the outline northward—
the nose, slightly curved; the chin, pure and
rounded; the bosom; the folded hands and
then a long stretch for the limbs; and at last,
far away, the upturned feet. You cannot help
seeing it; it is all so plain and so beautiful."

With a puzzled look old Guldbrand followed
the direction of the boy's finger, and evidently
made an honest effort to comprehend him. But
at last he gave an impatient toss of his head
and said:

"There is no face there, you lunatic! And
there you stand and dare to make a fool of
your father. I will teach you to try that
again."

With this warning he gave the astonished
boy a box on the ear which felled him to the
ground. For the old man was strong, and his
wrath was not to be trifled with.

"Get up," he cried, as the boy made no motion to rise. But the son did not stir.

"Get up, I say," roared the father a second
time, lifting the lad by the shoulders and
placing him upon his feet. But as he met his

eye, in which burned for a moment a wild passion of hate, he dropped him suddenly and walked into the house. He did not know how grievously he had wounded him; he did not know that he had violated his holy of holies.

Ingolf did not weep, as he lay there in the grass. Wild thoughts wrestled in his mind. An hour passed and the dew began to fall, but he did not stir. The sun was hidden, but its rays still slanted through the upper air and spread a luminous shimmer downwards. Then footsteps were heard, and Ingolf felt a warm hand upon his head. He looked up and saw the schoolmaster.

" It is damp to lie in the grass now," said he, kindly.

" I don't care if it is," answered Ingolf.

"Things have gone wrong, I perceive," remarked the schoolmaster with a smile which was both insinuating and sympathetic.

" So they have," said the boy, raising himself on his elbows.

" And I don't suppose I could help you? "

" I don't think you could—unless—unless— "

the boy hesitated, gazing intently into the schoolmaster's wrinkled and kindly face; "unless," he continued, "you could tell me whether you have ever seen the mountain maiden."

"The mountain maiden!" exclaimed the schoolmaster with a startled look. "No, I never saw her."

"I will show her to you," said the boy, seizing him by the arm, and pointing with eager gestures toward the chain of cliffs that dented the western horizon. He saw himself, plainly, the beautiful colossal maiden, outstretched in her strong slumber, and his eyes hung expectantly upon his teacher's face as if imploring him to see largely and clearly. Old Aslak, for that was the schoolmaster's name, adjusted his spectacles, three, four times carefully upon his hooked nose, but his expression grew more puzzled the longer he looked.

"You see nothing?" queried the boy with tears in his voice; "you cannot see the mountain maiden?"

"No, my boy, no," said the schoolmaster; "there is nothing there to see except a jagged chain of rocks ; and any one who says he sees anything else is a fool or a loon.   Have I not for seven-and-twenty years taught the youth of this valley their A B C, and the elements of the Christian faith as they are expounded in Dr. Martin Luther's little catechism ?   There is no one in the parish who knows more than I do, except the parson; and unless he sees your mountain maiden, I will swear that she is a phantasm of your own confused brain."

II.

ABOUT a month later, when the wheat was ripe, Ingolf was standing in the harvest field which was near to the highway. He had thrown his scythe upon the ground, and he held in his hand a blue corn-flower and a sprig of a weed which in Norway is called the wild mustard. Just at that moment the parson passed by. He was a stout and pompous man, who preached the crucifying of the flesh, but himself cared much for the good things of this world. Recognizing the handsome boy in the field he stopped and called him by name.

"What is that you are gazing at so intently, my lad?" asked he in a voice that rang from mountain to mountain.

Ingolf started and looked up blushing, as if he had been caught doing something wrong.

"O, I have so many strange thoughts," he murmured, in confusion.

"Well, let us hear your strange thoughts,"

said the parson cheerily, stepping across the ditch and walking close up to the boy.

"I was thinking—I was wondering," stammered Ingolf, "what kind of weeds the tares were which the enemy sowed in the wheat field, while the husbandmen were asleep. I have noticed that the corn-flower and the wild mustard always grow in wheat fields, but I have never noticed any other weed in great numbers, except the poppy. Could it be possible that these pretty flowers have been sown by the enemy?"

"The Scriptures say that the enemy sowed *tares*," said the parson solemnly.

"But I don't know what tares are; I supposed it meant a weed."

The parson stood for a moment pondering; he had preached at least twenty times on the parable of the tares among the wheat, but it had never occurred to him to associate any plant of definite form and color with the Biblical weed.

"You should not inquire into those things which the Lord has hidden from us," he remarked, gravely.

" But why should the Lord hide from us so many things which it would benefit us to know ? " asked the boy, innocently.

" Child, child ! " exclaimed the clergyman, " the enemy has been sowing his tares in your own mind. These wicked thoughts, this spirit of self-righteousness, this questioning the wisdom of God and of God-given authorities, these are the most dangerous tares that flourish in the fields of youthful minds at the present day. Therefore, if you would have His good wheat thrive and grow fertile in your soul, cease questioning, and believe."

The boy was completely overawed. He dropped the flowers reluctantly and seized the scythe.

" That is right," cried the parson ; " work and pray that ye fall not into temptation. In the sweat of thy brow shalt thou eat thy bread. Work is the right antidote against dangerous thoughts."

He turned on his heel and was about to continue his walk when his eyes fell upon the pretty corn-flowers. With much difficulty he stooped and began to pick them up. Their vivid color and singular shape interested him. "These do not grow in Palestine," he muttered, as if speaking to himself; "and the tares certainly must have been an Asiatic weed."

Ingolf paused in his work and listened again eagerly. He had a bright and easily impressible mind, in which joy and pain followed each other in quick succession. At the pastor's words his face lighted up with pleasure.

"What is it now which excites you?" queried the minister, somewhat impatiently.

"Oh, it pleased me to know," answered the boy, half bashfully, "that the Lord is not stern enough to throw these bright flowers into the fire on the last day."

"You foolish boy, you foolish boy," said the parson in a gentler mood, patting him softly on the shoulder. "The Lord is terrible only to sinners and idlers who speculate instead of following his command to Adam, which I have just quoted to you. It is those who are meant by the tares which are to be cast into the fire."

This friendly didactic tone was so encouraging that the desire arose in Ingolf's mind to submit to the pastor's decision the one ever-present thought which haunted him. If the pastor, who was the wisest man in the parish, could not see the mountain maiden, then it was evident that the schoolmaster was right, that the large, placid image was but a delusion of his disordered brain. But as he looked toward the mountains and saw the beautiful genius of his life outstretched in majestic repose, he prayed earnestly that the Lord would open the pastor's eyes, so that he might be able to see the mountain maiden. His heart beat violently, as he approached the minister with his eyes fixed imploringly upon his face, and the momentous question trembled upon his lips.

"Mr. Pastor," he began—but his voice shook and the tears nearly choked him—"Mr. Pastor, can you see the mountain maiden?"

"The mountain maiden?" cried the pastor in visible alarm.

"Yes; the great stone face now looming

against the sunset and the beautiful bosom and the folded hands? "

The tears now burst forth and he flung himself down in the stubble, crying with a piteous voice : " Oh, you cannot see her, you cannot see her ? "

" The boy is mad," grumbled the pastor, as he walked back to the highway ; " I certainly must speak to his father."

III.

THREE days passed during which Ingolf never once looked toward the mountain maiden. When the longing drew him he turned his head resolutely away and whistled wildly in order to divert his thoughts. The dread of insanity stood constantly at his mind's door and knocked unceasingly, demanding admittance. But he fought it off with the strength of despair, and wept and prayed with a frantic energy. And yet the very moment his soul rebounded into its natural attitude he saw in spirit the colossal maiden sleeping under the spacious sky. No force of prayer or tears could obliterate her image from his mind : even though he might persuade himself that she had no existence, since so wise and pious a man as the parson had failed to see her, his memory still protested against the enforced belief.

174

In the heat of his conflict Ingolf had sought refuge in the birch grove, about a mile from the house. There he sat upon a large moss-grown stone and saw the sunshine quiver in the air, and heard the whirring of the crickets in the grass. A terrible desire had taken possession of him to look but once more westward—only once more—and exchange a farewell greeting with the mountain maiden. The desire pursued him, and he had to press his face down into the moss in order to resist it. It seemed to him a temptation of the evil one, and the beautiful stone maiden became an image of dread, associated in some inexplicable manner with evil powers which strove to lead him away from God. But, for all that, she was no less tempting, no less beautiful. With a wild, unthinking energy, only to keep the tempter at bay, he repeated "Our Father," and his young voice sounded strangely amid the bird song and the whisper of the wind in the tree-tops; but gradually the voice grew fainter, and the whisper of the wind grew into a soft, unceasing song, and the birds and the crickets paused to listen. There was a great rushing sound under the heavens, and the mountain maiden opened her eyes and rose, large and beautiful, looming with her head and her ample shoulders into the clear, sun-teeming sky. Ingolf forgot to pray, and gave a loud, joyous shout which echoed from mountain to mountain. And he saw her walking grandly over the earth, and the tranquil majesty of her face was inconceivable. In her hands, which he now for the first time saw unfolded, she held a common stone, a clod of earth, a bunch of fresh grass, and a snake, upon whose coiled body shone in golden letters the legend, "The knowledge of good and evil." She came nearer and nearer, and stooped down over the boy and lifted him in her large arms until his vision soared through the boundless space, and he breathed an air that was intoxicatingly sweet and pure. His whole being seemed to be throbbing with joy; he had never been so happy in all his life. She bore him toward a distant mountain and placed him upon its pinnacle, whence his vision had a full sweep of the earth and the sky. There she gave him the handful of earth, the stone, the blades of grass and the snake, saying, "Sing of these." But when she turned her back, and was about to move away, he clung to her arm, crying, "Oh, stay with me!" She shook her head, and answered, "I shall return."

A harsh scream close to his ear brought him to his feet. He was still in the birch grove, and the crickets were singing about him; but a hawk was sitting upon a low bough of the birch under which he had been lying, and the birds were silent. He stared about him with dazed eyes. He did not know whether he had been awake or dreaming.

In the joy of this memory the days passed rapidly, and the summer drew toward its end. The English and American tourists who climbed the mountains and forded the seething rivers during the warm months began to turn their flight, with the other birds of passage, southward. Then, as the vision faded, and the doubts reasserted themselves, the old sorrow returned.

12

It was during one of the long, sunny days of the late autumn that a beautiful lady came to the farm and asked if she could get a change of horses. Her carriage, too, was slightly out of gear and needed mending. Ingolf saw her standing in the middle of the lawn before the house, and he gave a great cry and flung himself at her feet. She stooped down over him and asked him in a kindly voice what ailed him; but he only stared with a wild fascination at her beautiful face and gave no answer.

"There is something strange in this," she said, smiling, "something which I do not understand. Do I remind you of any one who is dear to you?"

Then he suddenly found his voice, and answered, "You are the mountain maiden who promised to return to me."

"The mountain maiden?" she repeated with a sweet, musical laugh. "Who is that?"

"Look!" he said, pointing with happy confidence toward the western mountain chain, "do you see the beautiful face gazing against the sky, the folded hands, the large bosom, and the feet? It is yourself; it is your face."

She gazed for a moment wonderingly, and her eyes grew grave, almost solemn.

"You are right," she said; "I see your mountain maiden; I think I can see the resemblance. You are a strange boy, but I like you. Tell me something about yourself."

He seated himself on the grass, and, while she waited, sitting under the drooping birch-tree, he told her the story of the mountain maiden.

"Ah!" she exclaimed, running her fingers caressingly through his hair, "you are a poet. You see what commonplace mortals cannot see."

"Yes," he said, mournfully, "I know I am something strange."

"And we will make you something great," she said, joyously. "Your trust in the mountain maiden shall not deceive you. Come with me to the city, and I will give you teachers and show you the great world. I'll ask your father to lend you to me for twelve years. Will you come?"

"I will follow you wherever you take me," he answered, while a strange radiance spread over his countenance.

IV.

THE twelve years passed, and a great poet appeared in the North—a poet who sang of the grand creation's chain; of the earth and her teeming life; of the vast processes of her growth; of the reign of law and order and progress. And he sang, not like the ancient declaimers, who saw but the surface of things, but as one having deep knowledge as well as power. Some called him a great man of science, others called him a mighty poet; but others again called him the enemy of mankind, the ruthless iconoclast, the Antichrist concerning whom John had prophesied in the Apocalypse. But the nation listened to him, and the lovers of liberty over the whole world heard his voice.

It was on the very day when the twelfth year was at an end that Ingolf and his foster-mother arrived in the valley; the peasants met them with music and speeches at the railroad station, and they drove in state to the old homestead where the poet's father, the pastor and the schoolmaster stood ready to receive them. Old Guldbrand was very feeble, and could not drive to the station.

"And do you remember twelve years ago," said the schoolmaster, when the preliminary greetings were over, "how you used to talk to me about the mountain maiden?"

"Whom you could not see," said Ingolf, laughing.

"I beg your pardon, sir," cried the schoolmaster, apparently much offended; "I saw the mountain image as plainly as I do you at this moment. Why, do you suppose I am blind?"

"Why, certainly, it is as plain as day," ejaculated the pastor, turning his rubicund face toward the west and tracing the outline of the imposing figure with his forefinger. "I always wondered at nature's consistency in having conformed so accurately to the human form."

"And you, too, father; do you see it?" asked Ingolf in amazement.

"What do you take me for, son?" asked the

old man with an incredulous mien; "why, I never remember the time when the thing wasn't perfectly plain to me. You don't suppose I came into the world blind, like a puppy?"

Ingolf was too happy to make a bitter reply; and yet bitter memories rose in his mind. But his foster-mother, divining his thought, drew him gently aside, and said:

"It is your glory that these men imagine they have always seen. The truth is no man's property, not even his who first sees it."

"You are right, as always," said Ingolf, kissing his foster-mother's brow. And they turned both, as with one accord, toward the west, where the mountain maiden lay, tracing her grand outline against the sunset.

A DANGEROUS VIRTUE.

A DANGEROUS VIRTUE.

I.

THERE was a great commotion down on the beach. Eight large boats, heavily freighted with boxes and chests, were lying at the point of the pier. The oarsmen were already in their places, lifting their dripping oars, and waiting for the last emigrants to embark. Out in the middle of the fiord the steam-boat was puffing and rumbling and shrieking, and now and then sending clouds and rings of steam up against the spotless blue sky. The mountains, black and solid at the base, rose through a hundred wondrous gradations of color and lightness to a height where their granite outlines seemed to dissolve into the pale-green, sunsteeped ether. Precipitate brooklets plunged down their sides, and traced their white paths

187

of foam against the dark stone ; but they seemed so infinitely remote, and their voices were lost in the vast calm which rested upon earth and sky. God's hand was invisibly outstretched in benediction over the pure and perfect day. The fiord, reflecting in its placid mirror the cool depths of the heavens, shut in on all sides by the gigantic mountain peaks, shivered now and then into trembling undulations whenever a sea-bird grazed its surface, and broke in pleasant, rhythmic ripples over the white sand.

At last all the boats were filled with emigrants. Only one belated straggler was still standing on the steps leading down to the water, gazing with tear-filled eyes into the face of a young woman, whose hands were tightly clasped in his own. He was a tall, blonde man of athletic build, with a frank, sun-burned face, and a pair of deep-set, serious blue eyes. There was an expression of determination, perhaps of obstinacy, in his roughly hewn features, and yet there was something sweet and tender lurking somewhere under the rugged surface, softening the harsh effect of nature's hasty workmanship.

The young woman, too, was tall and fair, and of fine proportions; her face was round and dimpled, and had that kind of rudimentary beauty which is so frequent among the Norse peasantry. She had a baby of about five months old strapped over her back, and gazed every now and then over her shoulder, whenever the pudgy little hands in their aimless gesticulations touched her ears or cheeks.

"You will be sure to come for me next year, Anders," she said, bursting into a fresh fit of weeping. "It will be so hard for me to be left· here all alone, and you wandering through the world without me. You know you never were a good hand at taking care of yourself, Anders. And your clothes will need mending, too. Oh, dear me, what will you do, Anders, without me?"

"It will be hard for me to get along without you, Gunhild," he answered, sadly. "But what should I do with you and the baby, as long as I have no house and home? The first year in

America is uncommonly hard, they tell me, and I would rather spare you, Gunhild, and take you into a warm, snug home, where you and the baby will find peace and comfort. In the meanwhile, Thorkel has promised to take care of you for a year, and if I do not come myself for you, there will be many friends going who will protect you from harm during the voyage."

"And your fifteen hundred dollars, Anders—don't you tell anybody that you have got it on your person. They might kill you, and then I should never see you again, and the baby would have no father any more. And don't ·you forget that I put your clean linen on the top in your chest, and your Sunday clothes in the right corner, directly under the hymn-book and the fine shirts."

"No, no, I shall forget nothing. And now, God bless you, wife. Let me kiss the baby. Take good care of him, and be sure you teach him to say 'father.'"

The blonde emigrant here stooped and rubbed his cheek against that of the diminutive mummy which was fighting in the air and cooing contentedly on its mother's back. "The little rascal!" said the father, with a faint smile. "He doesn't know that his father is to leave him for so long a time. Give me your hand, baby dear," he continued, addressing himself to the infant, "and take good care of your mother while I am gone."

He turned resolutely about and descended the stairs; but, on the last step, he lingered, turned his head once more, and leaped up on the pier. They made a fine group, those two, clasping each other's hands, with the sunlit air about them, the glittering fiord beneath them, and the white sea-gulls circling above them.

The steamer gave three long shrieks, the oarsmen shouted, and the sea-birds, as if to increase the general commotion, screamed wildly as they rose from the water and drifted in snowy masses through the clear air. The belated emigrant stumbled down the steps and flung himself into the stern of the last boat.

II.

ANDERS GUDMUNDSON RUSTAD was the youngest son of a well-to-do peasant in Hardanger, on the western coast of Norway. His father, who, during his life-time, had been a magnate in the parish, had left a large farm to be divided among his three sons; and the sons had scrupulously carried out his last instructions regarding the property, and had striven bravely to maintain themselves and their families on their divided patrimony; but it was a hard struggle, and experience taught them daily that without any capital to invest in houses and improvements, their lives would be a continual hand-to-hand battle with poverty. What was worse, they could no longer hope to assert the traditional influence of their family in parochial affairs, and they foresaw the time when their name would no longer be as weighty and as honored as it had been in ages past. The three brothers, therefore, held a family council in order to determine what measures should be taken to uphold the honor and authority of their ancient name. They were all three rigidly honest, upright, and law-abiding men, and one was as well qualified as another to wield the influence which had belonged to each generation of their race as by ancient right. They were, moreover, men of a strongly moral bias— grave, thoughtful, and tenacious of their purpose when once they had shaped their course of action. When the day for the family council arrived, each had, therefore, pondered out his own solution of the all-important problem, which he clung to with unwavering energy, and it was only after a long and hard-fought competition in generosity that Anders's plan prevailed, and his eldest brother, Thorkel, as the legitimate representative of the family, determined to accept his self-sacrifice in the name of his race. It was only just and fair, Anders argued, that when a younger brother, by his mere existence, interfered with the best interests of the family, he should seek for himself a new sphere of activity, and remove to

13

fresh fields of labor. By a continual subdivision of the land between the descendants of each new generation, the mightiest race would gradually degenerate into mere tenants and day-laborers, and the influence built up by prudent and laborious ancestors would be squandered and uselessly dissipated by short-sighted and improvident descendants. In order not to cripple his eldest brother in his efforts to assert his influence and independence, Anders volunteered to accept a mere nominal sum—one thousand dollars—as a compensation for his share in the landed inheritance, and, with this, and the five hundred more which belonged to his wife, he hoped to found a new home in America, and to establish for himself an honored and influential name in the great western hemisphere. This was no hasty conclusion which he uttered on the spur of the moment. For two years past he had studied the English language, the pronunciation of which he had learned from an English lord whose guide he had been on his hunting and fishing expeditions for several summers.

The second son, Björn, not wishing to be outdone in generosity by his younger brother, accepted a similar compromise, and, having a turn for trade, resolved to settle in one of the cities on the sea-coast as a lumber-dealer. It was agreed, however, that Anders's wife and child should remain at the old homestead until he should have succeeded in making the proper arrangements for their reception in his new home beyond the sea.

It was the middle of April, 186–, when Anders landed at Castle Garden. His fifteen hundred dollars he had sewed up securely in a leathern belt, which he wore about his waist, next to the skin. Nevertheless, the purser on the steamboat divined that he carried a large sum of money on his person, and, beckoning him aside, warned him, in a friendly whisper, against the dangers to which an immigrant exposed himself by being his own banker. He begged him to hasten to deposit his money in a safe bank, where he could draw it at will, and where, moreover, he would get interest on that part of it which he might not immediately use.

The Norseman, who had not let the least hint
fall concerning his wealth, was not a little
alarmed at the purser's power of divination,
and, although saying nothing, resolved on the
spot to follow his advice. He dared consult no
one, having a natural distrust of foreigners,
and believing, as most Norsemen do, that the
principal occupation of Americans consists in
outwitting the more innocent and unsophisti-
cated nations of the earth. Having intrusted
his luggage to the agent of the steamship
company, he launched forth boldly, with the
intention of taking a promenade through the
city, and obtaining a preliminary survey of it
before selecting a temporary place of lodgings;
but hardly had he emerged from the gate of
Castle Garden, before he was hailed by a dozen
frantic men, some of whom recommended obscure hotels, with much feverish eloquence,
while others greeted him as an old, long-lost
friend, and insisted upon overwhelming him with
affectionate attentions. To our Norseman, who
had always looked upon himself and been looked upon by others as a man of shrewdness and

authority, it was very humiliating to be selected
as an easy prey by these importunate rogues.
He had always felt himself firm and free, with
his foot planted on his native rock, and it gave
him, in this moment, an unpleasant shock to be
placed at a disadvantage by creatures of an in-
ferior species. To them, he reflected hurriedly,
his ancient name was but an unmeaning, bar-
baric sound, and it was folly to attempt to assert an authority which no one recognized; he
therefore extricated himself as best he could
from the crowd, being conscious of a vague uneasiness and annoyance, and dreading to use
his superior strength lest he might offend
against the unknown laws of this enigmatical
country. The noise about him grew more and
more deafening. To his ears, accustomed only
to the murmur of the sea and the scream of the
eagle in the vast solitudes, this incessant tramp
of feet, the harsh rattle of wheels upon the
stone pavements, and the shouts of men in
strange tongues, were so utterly bewildering
that he had frequently to pause to collect his
senses, and his reason seemed to be wandering

beyond his control. His firm confidence in himself as a normal and well-regulated human being began, for the first time in his life, to desert him. His Norse costume, which he had worn since the days of his childhood, and the propriety of which he had never thought of questioning, now suddenly appeared queer and outlandish ; and the half-curious, half-contemptuous glances which he received from the men and women who hurried past him, made him alternately burn and shiver, until he only longed to hide himself in some dark and quiet place where no human eye could reach him. He trembled at the thought that perhaps these strange people, with their keen unsympathetic eyes, had, like the purser on the ship, discovered that he carried a large sum of money in his belt, and were only watching their opportunity to take it away from him. The weight of the gold eagles seemed to be dragging him down; his knees shook under him, and his blood throbbed in his ears and temples until he feared to take another step, lest he should fall to the ground and be trampled down by the unfeeling multitude that were pressing about him on all sides. At this moment, just as his strength was on the point of failing him, his eyes fell, as if by chance, upon a huge stone building, upon the front of which was written, in large, gilt letters, "Immigrants' Savings Bank and Trust Company." The word "immigrant" first caught his glance, and by means of the pocket-dictionary which he carried with him he easily made out the meaning of the rest. This was evidently a hint of Providence. An Immigrants' Savings Bank and Trust Company! The latter half of the title, especially, appealed to him; it had such an assuring sound —a Trust Company! The very name inspired confidence. It was exactly the kind of institution which he wanted.

The weary and bewildered Norseman straightened himself up; he took off his cap and ran his hand through his blonde hair. The cool air blew against his throbbing forehead, and he drew a full, long breath, and reflected that, after all, the God of the Norseman could see him even in this remote and tumultuous world, and would not desert him. So he whispered a snatch of an old hymn, and hastened across the street toward the huge granite edifice, which he stopped once more to admire. Surely here was something solid and tangible ; no flimsy ornaments, no whimsical striving for originality in design ; everywhere square blocks of stone, with an air of stability and grave decorum about them which left no room for doubt as to the civic weight and responsibility of the men who had erected them. And, as if to dispel the last shadow of a misgiving that might still be lingering in the depositor's mind, they had had their names engraved in neat gilt letters upon the granite bases of the pillars which supported the lofty, round-arched portico of the entrance to the bank. The simple Norseman took his cap clean off, and held it respectfully in his hand, while he contemplated the ponderous respectability of these euphonious syllables. " Hon. Randolph Melville, sr., President " ! Who would deny that there was something fine and alluring in the very sound of that name ? Mr. Randolph Melville was Honorable—that was a matter of course to the immigrant's mind; for he knew not the cheapness of that frequently so ironical title in the United States, nor did he know the processes by which it is acquired. It seemed more significant to him that Mr. Randolph Melville was the senior of that name, and he immediately pictured to himself the honorable bank president as a white-haired patriarch, surrounded by an admiring and affectionate family, who looked to him for counsel and guidance. With this pleasing picture hovering before his mind, he resolutely entered the bank and placed his cap upon the snow-white marble counter. Behind the little windows half a dozen clerks, with rigidly neutral countenances, were scribbling away busily, and hardly deigned to notice the rustic, who, with the air of a humble petitioner, was wandering from one window to another, and endeavoring to attract their distinguished attention. Finally, a very elegantly attired little man, with an exquisite black mustache, inclined his head slightly towards an opening which bore the inscription,

"Receiving Teller," and, without responding to the Norseman's respectful greeting, asked him, in a gruff voice, what he wanted.

"I have fifteen hundred dollars," faltered Anders, in indifferent English, "and I should like to deposit it here for some months, until I shall need it."

The teller, instead of answering, bent once more over his books, as if he had heard nothing.

"I have fifteen hundred dollars——" began the immigrant once more ; but the teller scribbled away for dear life, and only stopped occasionally to wipe his forehead with a white handkerchief.

At this moment a tall, majestic-looking man, with iron-gray hair and a handsome, clean-shaven face, entered from an inner room and approached the counter.

"What does this man want?" he said, confronting the clerk with a gaze of withering severity.

"He wants to make a deposit, sir," answered the clerk.

"What is your name, my good fellow?" asked the majestic man, in a tone of benign condescension.

"Anders Gudmundson Rustad," replied the Norseman, cheerfully. He felt sure that this was the Hon. Randolph Melville, sr., and he reflected with satisfaction that his actual appearance differed but slightly from the imaginary portrait of him which he had constructed at the sight of his name.

"And what is the amount you wish to deposit?" inquired Mr. Melville, seizing a small pasteboard book from a pile which was neatly stacked under the counter.

"Fifteen hundred dollars. It is all I possess in this world—my own inheritance and that of my wife."

"Yes, yes, I understand," said the banker, impatiently. "Hand it here, please."

The immigrant unbuttoned his red waistcoat, unbuckled the heavy leathern belt, and cut the seam open at one end with his knife. He then counted out the large, shining gold pieces upon the counter, whereupon Hon. Randolph

Melville pushed them with an indifferent, business-like air into an open drawer, and handed the depositor the little book through the window.

"We pay five per cent," he said, "and you can draw at pleasure."

"But," stammered the Norseman, who was gazing with a bewildered expression into his book, "I have only given you fifteen hundred, and here you have put down twenty-one hundred."

"Yes, gold is at a premium of forty per cent."

And Mr. Melville, with the same severe and majestic air, turned his back on his rustic interlocutor, and reëntered his private office. There were a dozen questions which Anders would have liked to ask regarding the best manner of drawing his money, etc., but he feared to trouble further the great man or his unresponsive clerks, and therefore betook himself away with a helpless mien and slow, reluctant steps. This world was a very puzzling affair after all, he reflected, and as for asserting the influence of the Rustad family and its Norse traditions in this chaotic whirlpool of conflicting interests, why, that was a hopeless undertaking.

III.

Anders Rustad, fearing to trust himself to the guidance of the hotel runners, returned that night to Castle Garden, where he slept on the floor of one of the galleries, with his jacket rolled up under his head for a pillow. Round about him, men and women in all sorts of curious costumes lay stretched out in sleep on boxes and trunks, and their heavy, regular breathing rose in a doleful chorus under the wide rotunda, and attuned his mind to melancholy reflections. He was half inclined to repent of the generous resolve by which he had voluntarily exiled himself from the ancient home of his race, and plunged rashly into a complex foreign world which he was ill qualified to cope with. And yet he argued to himself, it was but an act of justice, and not of generosity. If his brother had been in his place, would he not have done likewise? Surely he would have acted in the same spirit.

206

Then the thought came to him of his beautiful fair-haired wife, who was longing to share his fate in this new land, and of his little boy, who would grow up, perhaps, to be a powerful man, and 'would conquer wealth and influence here where there was yet elbow-room for every free and energetic spirit. He built in imagination, first, a snug little cabin, then a stately, spacious mansion upon the western prairie, and he saw his wife entering it for the first time, her fair face beaming with gratitude and pleased surprise. Happy visions floated before his closed eyes, and pursued him into that delightful state of semi-consciousness which precedes the dreamless slumber.

The next morning, Anders resolved to find the railroad depot and to start on his westward journey. He felt hopeful and strong, and was half ashamed of the weakness which he had shown the day before. The noise was now positively exhilarating; he had a sensation of being part of it, and it buoyed him up with joyous excitement. The pulse of the world was beating vigorously, and its strong life-currents were beginning to circulate through his own being. The tall, blank-looking edifices from which men kept running out and in, like bees at the mouth of a hive, looked far less forbidding than the day before; their unindividualized severity had, at all events, acquired the dignity of a useful purpose. The sunlight was pouring in a mild, steady stream into the broad thoroughfare; the chimes of Trinity were ringing merrily through the clear air; and the men who were every moment alighting from the crowded omnibuses, with the morning papers in their hands, had an air of self-confidence and success which was almost inspiring. All that a sensible and industrious Norseman required, in order to conquer a place for himself in this bright and busy land, was a little spiritual acclimatization, and that the years would imperceptibly supply without much conscious effort. I am not sure that Anders's meditations on this subject were clearly formulated in the above phrases, but he had a cheerful sense that his foreignness was gradually wearing away, and that within a short time he would be able to engage in the struggle for existence on equal terms with his fellow-competitors.

While pursuing these pleasant fancies, Anders had reached the corner of the street where the bank reared its stately façade against the blue sky. A dense crowd of excited people, mostly laborers in fustian and shabbily attired women, were gathered about its closed doors, and four policemen were striving in vain to clear the sidewalk and to open a passage for the constantly growing throng of pedestrians. Half a dozen horses, harnessed to enormous drays, were plunging and rearing in the middle of the street, and the drivers were swearing and cracking their whips, while freshly arriving vehicles, with difficulty detained by the policemen, every moment increased the tumult and confusion. Our Norseman, to whom this was a novel, and, on the whole, an entertaining spectacle, rushed forward to assist in disengaging the interlocked wheels, and by two vigorous pulls succeeded in setting one of the drays at liberty.

14

The driver, without stopping to thank him, whipped up his horses and drove off at a rapid trot; the other teams followed, and within a minute the traffic of the street had resumed its usual noisy regularity. Anders, who had hardly had time to wonder at the presence of the crowd, and still less at its fierce excitement, supposing both to be normal phenomena of American life, now respectfully approached a policeman and asked him, in his broken English, if any calamity had happened, and why the people appeared so agitated.

"The bank is busted," replied the officer, laconically.

"Busted?" asked the Norseman, with a vague sense of alarm; for the word "busted" did not exist in his vocabulary.

"Yes; gone up the spout," explained the officer, with a gruff laugh. "Gone where the woodbine twineth."

The immigrant was utterly mystified; by a violent effort he repelled the one rational explanation of the scene, and, clinging to a futile hope, hauled out his friend, the dictionary.

But neither the definition of "spout" nor of "woodbine" suggested the remotest clue to the enigma. Looking up, he saw a lean, middle-aged woman shaking her clenched fist in helpless rage against the broad stone façade of the building, which in its granite security seemed to smile defiance down upon her. Angry men were rushing up the front steps and hammering with their heels and elbows against the solid oak doors, while others were threatening the policemen, who were making a faint show of restraining them from further violence. Anders stood and gazed and gazed in numb, shivering silence. He was dimly aware that a great calamity had happened, and that it had happened to him; but the shock had paralyzed his thoughts, and his mind seemed a cold vacuum. He felt a dull throbbing in his head and a strange numbness in his limbs. He heard the screams and curses around him as one hears voices in a dream; the sunlight poured down upon him, but it was no longer the same sunlight he had rejoiced in but a few moments ago; it was rather like something white

and heavy—a bright and dense veil, which fell
with a positive weight upon his eyes. The
crowd now filled the whole street; two or
three stones were flung against the windows of
the bank; then some one climbed up on the
front steps and gesticulated wildly, while ap-
pearing to speak, though no one appeared to
hear what he said. Suddenly, in the midst of
all this tumult, Anders felt himself hurried
away by an impulse which he was powerless
to resist. He heard a rhythmic tramp of feet,
the report of one or two pistols, and saw
the multitude scattering in precipitate haste
through the neighboring streets.

When he had regained control of his senses,
he found himself sitting on a bench in the
square in front of the City Hall. A brooding
calm had come over him, and he saw with
painful vividness the consequences of the calamity which had overtaken him. Where were
now the home on the prairie, his son's future,
and his wife's joyous surprise? A sense of injury, mingled as yet with sorrow for those that
were dear to him, kept burrowing more and

more deeply into his soul; and as he recalled
the scenes of yesterday—the majestic indifference of the thief and his own humility—keen-
er pangs awoke within him, and he sprang up
and shook his clenched fists against the heavens. If there was a righteous God sitting
there above, how, then, could such a monstrous wrong be possible? And, if he was
deaf to the cries of the oppressed, was it not
then the duty of the wronged man to take the
judgment into his own hands, and to help
himself to justice? The justice of this world
was for the great, not for the small. How
could he now, without money or influence,
without friends or connections, obtain the
means to prosecute before a court of law the
robber who had stolen his happiness, his
future, and his very faith in God away from
him? He remembered well that the venerable
preacher at home promised the righting of all
wrongs in the hereafter, and that arrangement
had always, up to the present moment, seemed
in a general way quite satisfactory. He had
never seen any reason why the injured man

should not be content to bide his time, and then, in the blessed security of Abraham's bosom, rejoice in the torments of Dives in the bottomless pit. But now, in that sudden clearance of vision which often follows in the wake of a great disaster, when the mightily aroused passion flings its fierce light into every corner of the soul, he saw how vague and also how unworthy of a just man was the hope of such a retribution. With every passing instant his horizon seemed to widen; the world re-adjusted itself in his mind according to new and hitherto unsuspected laws, and he saw and felt things which he had never seen and felt before. A burning unrest possessed him, and he hungered for action of some mighty sort. The mere personal wrong had suddenly assumed relations to the world at large, with its hoary abuses, and he yearned to seize hold of its hidden levers and cogwheels, and to set the universe right.

While these defiant thoughts were rushing through his brain, Anders was moving rapidly across the square, talking aloud to himself, and stopping every now and then to shake his fist at some invisible antagonist. Though at first bewildered by the newness and the noisy commotion of the great city, he was at heart no milksop, and now that the slumbering strength of his Norse nature had been aroused, the tempest within him was not easily stilled. He saw all that went on around him, but only in a remote and misty way, and he felt a sort of fierce satisfaction amid all his misery that now at last he saw things as they actually were. He pitied his old simple self, and thought of his old contented life with affectionate contempt.

The sun rose higher in the heavens, the day advanced ; and still he kept marching up one street and down another, feeling no weariness, but only a feverish need of moving. It was a little after noon that he paused by accident before a sooty-looking building, over the door of which the coat-of-arms of the United Scandinavian kingdoms was displayed. He read the name of the Norwegian consul on a sign attached to one of the steps of the stairs, and

yielding to a momentary impulse he entered
the office. It might be well not to leave any
stone unturned in his efforts to obtain justice.
The consul was a tall, well-built man, of stately
presence, and with a kindly and refined face.
He rose from his seat and received the immigrant with courtesy, as if he had been a high
functionary of state. There was something in
the peasant's bearing and manner which instantly commanded respect.

"Take a seat," said the consul, inviting Anders to step within the railing which divided
the inner sanctuary of the office from the part
accessible to the public. "I see by your face
that you have something important to say to
me."

"So I have, Mr. Consul," said Anders,
"though I hardly expect you can do much for
me."

And he told simply and straightforwardly
what had befallen him, since he landed, up to
the present moment.

"H'm, h'm; that is a bad story," said the
consul; "but whatever I can do for you shall

certainly be done. It is unfortunately not an
international affair in which your Government
can interfere."

"And what would you advise me to do, Mr.
Consul?" asked the immigrant, laying both his
hands weightily on his knees.

"I would advise you to write to the corporation——"

"The corporation—what is that?"

"A corporation," responded the consul, with
a hesitating smile,—"well, a corporation is a
sort of composite creature, 'which has no body
to be whipped, and no soul to be damned.'"

"Then I am afraid there would be no use in
my writing to it."

"Well, then, I would write to the Hon. Randolph Melville, sr., personally, and state my
grievance plainly. He is a charitable person,
and would, perhaps, be induced to make an
exception in your favor."

Anders jumped up as if something had stung
him.

"Grievance! Charity!" he cried, indignantly.
"I do not ask charity, Mr. Consul—I demand

justice! Mr. Randolph Melville stole my money, knowing that it was all I possessed in this world, and knowing, too, that he would fail on the following day. Now, if there is justice to be had in this land, I want to have him punished."

"Aha! That is what you want!" exclaimed the consul. "Well, then, I am afraid I cannot help you. You must remember that Mr. Melville is not the bank; he is only its president, and he does not act without the knowledge and consent of the directors, who, naturally, are no more and no less guilty than he is himself. Perhaps you would like to see the whole company in jail in suits of striped garments?"

"I would; and it is no more than just that, if they are all guilty, they should all be punished."

"My dear fellow, I fear your sense of justice will be the ruin of you."

"I am willing to be ruined in so good a cause—that is, if I accomplish my end by my ruin."

"Heavenly powers!" cried the official. "What a fierce and unchristian temperament! If you had lived as long in this country, or, in fact, in this world, as I have, you would have learned that insisting so obstinately upon one's right is the surest road to destruction, temporal and eternal. Have we not all daily to accept compromises where, for some reason or other, it is impossible to obtain absolute justice? In fact, isn't our whole political life and our whole civilized society made up of compromises between right and wrong? Prudence dictates it; religion recommends and sanctions it. You know the parable of the unjust steward, and Christ's counsel to his disciples to make friends with the mammon of unrighteousness. Now, in your case, your duty is very simple. Probably within a few weeks a percentage of ten or fifteen cents on the dollar will be declared, and you will get your share. Put that in your pocket and start West, and do as well as you can with it."

Anders stood with his hand on the railing, listening in rebellious silence to what the consul said. To him such a compromise with evil was mean and cowardly, and utterly repugnant. No; he wanted justice, and the last drop of his blood he would stake in his efforts to obtain it.

"One thing more, Mr. Consul," he said, looking up into the latter's kindly face with his large serious eyes. "You know Mr. Randolph Melville?"

"I know him very well. I have known him for years."

"Where does he live?"

"Fifth Avenue. No. —."

"Thank you. And will he give up his fine house and have his furniture sold?"

"Good gracious, no! I am pretty sure he will not do that. The house, moreover, belongs to his wife."

"Then he married a rich wife?"

"No, not that exactly. She was quite poor when he married her, but she is very rich now."

"She has inherited money since she was married?"

"No; as far as I know, she has inherited nothing."

"How then has she gained her wealth?"

The consul shrugged his shoulders significantly.

"You should not inquire too curiously into family mysteries," he said, with a sardonic smile.   "It isn't right nor delicate."

There was a long pause, during which the consul sat tapping the corner of his desk meditatively with his gold pencil.

"If I accept nothing less than a hundred cents on the dollar," said Anders, at last, "what will happen then?"

"You will get nothing."

"Yes, something I shall get."

"And what is that?"

"Justice."

"That is a poor exchange for two hundred dollars."

The door opened and closed, and the heavy, determined steps of the immigrant sounded defiantly in the consul's ears.

"Poor fellow!" he sighed; "he will be sure to come to grief.   But for all that, one can't help admiring the fine stuff he is made of."

IV.

Society appears very different when looked at through one eye-glass from its topmost stratum, from what it does when looked at from its nether side through a haze of tears. To a man who can afford French cookery and champagne with his dinner, and who can arrange his comforts regardless of their expense, the ways of Providence are apt to seem just and good; while he who, since he committed the mistake of being born, has been tripped up at every step by fatal mischances, to whom the prospect of a dinner is always more or less problematic, and to whom physical comfort is an unknown quantity, is hardly to be blamed if he regards the existing order of things as being not entirely above criticism. I have heard people, who have been unacquainted with any severer hardship than dyspepsia after a too hearty meal, moralize blandly concerning the labor problem and the unwarrant-

222

able rebelliousness of the lower classes, and devise, in the abstract, delightfully inadequate remedies for the cure of the great social evils; but I have always suspected that a little concrete experience of misery would shake the basis of their reasoning, and, perhaps, bring about a radical reconstruction of their social philosophy.

Six weeks had passed since the failure of the "Immigrants' Savings Bank and Trust Company." During this time Anders Rustad had called almost daily at the house of Hon. Randolph Melville, sr., on Fifth Avenue, but he had never been admitted. The colored servant had at last rudely slammed the door in his face, as soon as he saw him, and told him that if he dared to come back his master would have him arrested. But Anders was nothing daunted; he had made up his mind to have an interview with Mr. Melville, and was resolved, if necessary, to persevere in his efforts to gain admission until the sounding of the last trump. He had, in the meanwhile, managed to subsist, after a fashion, on the little money he had obtained by the sale of his railroad ticket to Minnesota.

He had offered his case to a score of lawyers, all of whom he had bewildered by his inability to comprehend, or his unwillingness to abide by, that system of half-measures and compromises which is embodied in our criminal and civil legislation, and in some of our political institutions.

"A thing is either right," this poor benighted immigrant reasoned, "and then it ought to be upheld, defended, and protected; or it is wrong, and should be condemned, prosecuted, and punished. Right and wrong can never shake hands and march along through life, arm in arm. If Melville cheated me and robbed me of my money, which his clerk would not take, why then he should be locked up in jail, so that other poor immigrants may be protected against him, and not fall into the hidden trap which again he may dig at their feet."

Anders had grown strangely keen-sighted during these miserable six weeks; all the

powers of his hitherto dormant soul had been
awakened, and he felt himself growing in mental stature with every passing day. But the
feverish current of his thought had dried up
his blood and made his cheeks pale and hollow,
and his eyes large and brilliant. His disordered hair hung in tangled locks down over his
forehead, his beard grew in long tufts over his
cheeks and chin, and his intense yet absent-
minded expression had so completely changed
the look of his face that his own brother would
probably have passed him without recognition,
had chance led their paths together.

On the evening of May 25th, Anders trudged
as usual up the avenue, revolving in his mind
some plan for capturing an interview with his
slippery opponent. He instinctively tightened
his grip on his stout cane whenever an ingenious thought occurred to him, and now and
then he stopped to pound the pavement in
fierce satisfaction. He did not ring at the
front door this time, but he climbed the fence
to the back yard, and thence swung himself
up on the roof of a vine-entwined arbor, from

15

which, without difficulty, he could reach the dining-room window. It was seven o'clock. The evening was warm, and a great blaze of light streamed out from within through the half-opened window. He saw through the slats of the inside blinds a large company assembled at dinner, and Mr. Melville's massive neck and broad, majestic back almost within reach of his outstretched arm. Next to him sat a beautiful young lady in a cream-colored silk dress, and with a large bunch of pale yellow roses high up on her left shoulder. There was a delicately insinuating flattery in her smile as she turned her fair face toward Mr. Melville, and submitted her airy opinions to his weighty and substantial judgments.

"Really, I can't see why the laboring classes should always be so horrid and discontented," Anders heard her saying. "They have not our fine sensibilities, and they never have been accustomed to anything better than what they have; why, then, should they not accept their lot in a Christian spirit of submission, instead of continually grumbling against Providence

and raising the prices of dresses and everything by their stupid strikes?"

"You are entirely right, Miss Van Pelt,"
said Mr. Melville, while his lofty smile perceptibly relaxed. "It is what I have always
maintained—that the rebelliousness of the laboring classes is the direct result of the wide-
spread religious unbelief of our age. That is
what these scientific disorganizers have accomplished by their wicked speculations. I have
always been an adherent of the good, strong,
old-fashioned religions, with sharply defined
doctrines and tangible hells. I have myself
built a mission chapel at Five Points, and I
always subscribe liberally to such objects.
What we especially want is preachers of un-
questioned orthodoxy,—men who will lay down
plainly the doctrine of punishments and re-
wards, who will maintain strict discipline in
their flocks, and teach absolute submission to
the inscrutable ways of Providence."

Mr. Melville had delivered this little speech
in a clear and emphatic voice, and as he ceased
speaking and lifted a glass of sparkling cham-

pagne to his lips, an audible murmur of applause ran around the table.

Anders heard and understood nearly every word. He trembled and clung convulsively to the window-sill. There sat the thief, prosperous and honored, and upon his splendid board were heaped up the toil of a thousand crushed and miserable creatures, the hope and faith and happiness of the hungry, the needy, and the oppressed,—all to be devoured in a leisure hour by a company of idle triflers. It even seemed to Anders, as Mr. Melville raised his tall champagne-glass to his lips, that he was drinking down his wife's and his little son's future, and all that was dear and precious to him in this world. He clutched his cane more tightly, but still strove to restrain his fury.

At that moment a tall and corpulent man, who sat a few seats from the host, rose, with some slight difficulty, and demanded the privilege of expressing the sentiments which, he felt assured, animated every one present in this distinguished company. The waiters then began to skip around the table ; the corks popped in spite of the efforts of the gentlemen from Delmonico's to restrain their vivacity and the sparkling liquid sissed and foamed and bubbled, and threatened to overflow the finely ornamented rims of the Venetian glasses.

"Ladies and gentlemen," said the corpulent guest, "it is to-day the sixtieth birth-day of our honored host, Mr. Randolph Melville. In proposing the health of my esteemed friend, I shall take the liberty to call your attention to some of those eminent qualities by which he has gained a well-merited distinction during his long career of public and private usefulness. First, Mr. Melville was, from his very cradle, set apart for a business man. He is in that respect a typical American, and embodies in his talents and in his character the genius of our great and glorious republic. His fellowcitizens have always reposed the utmost confidence in him, and have honored him with a multitude of public trusts; and he has, by his uprightness and unfailing rectitude, amply justified their confidence. His has been a life shining brightly in the broad daylight of publicity," etc.

In this strain Mr. Melville's corpulent friend continued for more than fifteen minutes; neither he himself nor any one else seemed to suspect the faintest shade of irony in his sonorous periods. When he had finished, Mr. Melville rose to respond. His massive head, his clear, handsome features, the expanse of immaculate shirt-bosom which covered his broad chest,—all looked wonderfully impressive. The clatter of knives and forks, and the hum of vapid small-talk ceased; the gentlemen threw themselves back in their chairs, and the ladies, with much rustling of silk and satin, settled themselves into becoming attitudes of expectation.

"Ladies and gentlemen," began Mr. Melville, "it is with deep gratification, and yet with a vivid sense of my own unworthiness, that I have listened to the remarks of my esteemed friend, Mr. Gauntlet. I should, however, do myself an injustice were I to deny that I have always lived and acted in accord-

ance with the light that has been vouchsafed
me; and I have been fully convinced that the
misfortunes with which I have so recently
been visited have been the chastening discipline of a just Providence. And in this faith
——"

At that moment something heavy shook the
floor, and made the glasses on the table jingle;
before Mr. Melville had time to face more than
half about, two strong hands seized him by
the throat, and a hoarse voice shouted in his
ear, "You lie!" He saw a haggard face,
covered with a disorderly blonde beard, thrust
close up to his own, and he met the gaze of
two fierce blue eyes which burned with an un-
steady fire. The grip of the iron fingers tightened over his throat; the air grew black before his eyes; and in his struggle to free himself he ground under his heels the broken frag-
ments of the wine-glass which had fallen from
his hand. The male guests, who had been
half stunned by the suddenness of the attack,
now sprang to their feet and rushed to Mr.
Melville's assistance. One or two of the ladies

fainted, and others fled screaming to the remotest corner of the room, where they gathered in a promiscuous embrace, and stared with
fascinated fright at the struggle of the men.
Miss Van Pelt only had the presence of mind
to skip across the hall to Mr. Melville's private library, and to touch the electric knob
which communicated with the nearest police
station.

The floor was shaking; the great chandeliers
under the ceiling trembled; for a few moments
a dozen men were intertangled in an inextric-
able knot, which swayed to and fro, now toward the window, now toward the table, until
at last it fell in a heap at the foot of the marble mantel-piece. One after another rose pant-
ing, surveyed his disordered toilet in the long
mirrors, and muttered a half-suppressed oath
between his teeth. Only the two original com-
batants remained motionless; the Norseman
lay glaring about him in vague amazement; a
shiver ran through his frame; his fury was expended, and seemed to have utterly exhausted
him. Mr. Melville lay outstretched at his

side, drawing now and then a long shuddering breath, and closing his fingers with a convulsive clutch. Two or three of his guests were bending anxiously over him, unbuttoning his waistcoat, untying his neck-tie, and feeling his pulse. Presently three policemen entered; they lifted Anders up and hustled him roughly toward the door. He made no remonstrance; every impulse seemed dead within him; but suddenly, as they reached the threshold, he straightened himself up to his full height, shook his fist threateningly, and cried, hoarsely: " Give me my money back that you stole from me ! "

V.

FOR several months the Norseman remained in the Tombs. No one offered to go bail for him, nor did any one appear to bear witness against him. The monotonous routine of the prison and the degrading companionship with thieves and robbers wore out his hope and his courage, and left nothing but the indignation, burning with a dull but steady flame, within him. With his elbows propped on his knees, and his two hands clutching a tuft of hair on each side of his head, he sat the livelong day, pondering the deep problems of existence. With eager impatience he looked forward to the day of his trial; for then, at last, he should have the chance of lifting up his voice loudly so as to pierce the deaf ears of justice. He planned in his own mother tongue a tremendous arraignment, and several days passed before it occurred to him that American justice spoke and understood only English. Then, with a miserable sense of his helplessness, he paced the floor of his narrow cell, knocking at times with his forehead against the wall, but hardly conscious of the pain. He felt as if his thoughts were wandering beyond his control, and only when the rage blazed up wildly did it light the dark chambers of his brain and enable him to collect his forces for action. It was at such a moment that a key was heard clicking in the lock, and the consul entered, followed by one of the wardens.

"I have good news for you, Mr. Rustad," said the consul, cheerily, grasping Anders's listless hand. "You are at liberty to leave this place at once."

"But, but—the trial," remonstrated the prisoner in a husky whisper.

"There will be no trial," answered the consul, with the air of one giving a very satisfactory piece of intelligence. "There is no one to accuse you."

"Why, then, have I been imprisoned?"

"You know that as well as I do; and you ought to appreciate Mr. Melville's humane and merciful spirit in refusing to appear against you."

"I do not want mercy, but justice!' roared Anders, springing to his feet and shaking his huge fist in the consul's face. "I want a trial, and I want to shout my wrong in the ears of the whole world, and of God himself."

"Now, now, do be reasonable, Mr. Rustad," urged the consul. "Only think of the hundreds, if not thousands, of poor people who are in the same predicament as you are. And do they make such an ado about it? No; they pocket their ten per cent. which was declared yesterday, and thank God that anything is left to them."

"It is that very thought which maddens me," cried the Norseman, still in a frenzy of excitement. "Tell me where they are, these poor, deluded people. Let me find them, and I will shame them into a just and implacable indignation at their wrongs. I will make them blush at their paltry spirit in meekly accepting one dollar for every ten which was their due."

The consul's face betrayed his astonish-

ment. Was this the language of a simple, un-
taught peasant, who but half a year ago had
few thoughts beyond the common routine of
agricultural toil ?

"As your countryman, Mr. Rustad, and one
who wishes you well," he said, in a voice of
grave remonstrance, " allow me to implore you
to do as they have done. Accept your two
hundred dollars, which you can draw to-morrow, and go West."

Anders turned his back on the consul with
disdain.

" You will not listen, then, to the voice of
prudence," the latter continued, laying his
hand persuasively on the peasant's shoulder.

" No, I will not!" thundered the Norseman.
" I will not leave this place without a trial, and
I will accept nothing but justice."

The consul shrugged his shoulders, and then,
with a glance at the jailer, tapped his forehead
significantly. The jailer nodded as if to say
that he understood. Half an hour later, Anders was forcibly ejected from the Tombs.

VI.

HE stood for a moment, bewildered, in the glare of the daylight. A crowd of boot-blacks and ragged *gamins* surrounded him, pulled at his clothes, and jeered at him; but he hardly saw them. The intensity of his thought dulled the outer sense. Twice or thrice he shook his fist at the heavens, then suddenly started with a rapid, feverish stride toward Broadway, and then up toward the fashionable avenue. People who saw him turned to look after him; his gigantic size, his pale face, covered with a disorderly beard, and his lustrous eyes inclined every one to change his course rather than risk a collision. It was early in the afternoon when Anders, without having paused for one instant in his march, reached Mr. Melville's brown-stone palace on the avenue. A beautiful carriage was standing before the door, and the two coachmen, themselves as shiny and well-groomed as their horses, were seated with an air of severe propriety on the box. Casting them a glance, full of hate and contempt, Anders leaped up the front steps, just as Mr. Melville himself, with a whip in his hand, and in the jauntiest of English driving costumes, opened the door from within. Seeing the terrible Norseman before him, he raised his whip threateningly; an expression of anger or of terror, or of both, passed over his face, and he seemed on the point of beating a retreat. But suddenly his wrath overmastered his fear, and swiftly reversing his whip he brought down the butt-end with a vigorous blow on his opponent's head. Anders reeled, but, instantly recovering his equilibrium, he darted forward and planted his huge fist in the bankers forehead. It grew black before Mr. Melville's eyes; he tottered, and, in his effort to keep his footing, wheeled around toward the edge of the stone steps, and fell backward. It was all the work of one brief moment. The grooms scrambled down from their seats, but they came just a second too late to catch their master in his fall. The blood flowed from an ugly gash in his head; a convulsive movement ran through his frame; then his features stiffened. He was dead. Anders stood with folded arms at the top of the stairs and looked steadfastly down upon the prostrate form. He was conscious of no joy or exultation, but rather of a fierce contentment that justice at last had been satisfied. The world seemed for one moment right.

He had no thought of himself or of his own fate; it was the world's fate, and the fate of the millions who suffered, mutely and without thought of revenge—it was this which concerned him. He could have marched to the stake unquailingly while this mood lasted. When the policemen arrived, he followed them without resistance, and his simple dignity even commanded some degree of respect. The fever in his blood had cooled, and a great calm reigned in its place. But it was not of long duration. As soon as the heavy iron doors had closed upon him, and the daylight fell sparingly through the thick bars of the window-gratings, his mind resumed its former

intense activity, and all the problems of the
universe seemed to rush in upon him, crying
for a solution. Strange to say, the memory of
his dear ones at home was well-nigh oblite-
rated in his soul. It was the love of wife and
child which had driven him away from his
snug hearth and out into the merciless world,
and it was the thought of them which had
made his misfortune tenfold more cruel and ap-
palling. Now they seemed like a dim memory,
which had no longer the power to arouse him.
But the wrong, the brutal, fiendish wrong!—
this had become wife and child to him, and he
nursed it tenderly in his bosom.

The winter passed, and the day for the trial
was appointed. In the midst of his gloom he
looked forward to that day with triumphant
anticipation. He had spent the winter in dili-
gent study of English, and had drawn up a
document in that tongue, which was to be read
in the presence of the jury. It seemed to him
that its charges were unanswerable and its
logic irresistible; he even prided himself a little on the eloquence of certain passages from

16

which, especially, he promised himself a startling effect. He was yet confident that the abuses which he pointed out needed only to be generally known to be instantly rectified; and it hardly occurred to him that it was he himself, and not the dead man, who was to be tried. The consul had engaged a skillful lawyer to defend him, and even volunteered to bear part of the expense. They had agreed to set up the plea of insanity, and had appointed an interview with Anders at the prison, in order to ask some questions and to give him the necessary instructions. He was conducted into their presence by the jailer, who remained at the door while the conversation lasted.

"You have changed much during these months, Mr. Rustad," said the consul, after having introduced Mr. Runyon, the lawyer, "and not for the better; you should sleep more and think less. We are going to get you out of this scrape all right; you need have no fear."

"I have no fear, Mr. Consul," answered Anders, firmly.

"But you must follow our instructions implicitly," put in the lawyer, " or you may spoil everything. You know this is a matter of life and death."

"And what are your instructions?"

"In the first place, we have agreed that we have the best chance of success with the plea of insanity."

"Insanity?"

"Yes, insanity."

"And do you mean to say that I am insane?"

Anders took two long strides toward the lawyer, who lifted his arms, as if in defence, and retreated toward the wall. The guard rushed forward, seized the Norseman by the shoulder, and pulled him back.

"Now, now, my dear Mr. Rustad," cried the consul, "you must keep your temper under control, or we shall never get along."

The lawyer again, though with an uneasy air, resumed his seat at the consul's side at the table.

"As I was saying," he began, playing nervously with his pencil, "it is not the question whether the consul and I believe you insane. Of course, between us, we do not. But the important point is to persuade the jury that you are insane."

The consul, who was anxiously watching the prisoner, observed again a threatening look in his eyes, and made haste to interpose :

"You understand, Mr. Rustad," he said, in his pleasant, soothing voice, "that the laws of this country require peculiar means to be resorted to, and I solemnly assure you that the plea of insanity (which, in your case, can very easily be defended) is your only escape from the gallows."

"If it is just that I die, then let me die," answered the peasant, calmly. "But I will not owe my life to a lie."

The lawyer, still playing with his pencil, leaned over toward the consul and whispered in his ear. The consul nodded, then said aloud:

"Well, Mr. Rustad, we have done the best we can for you. If you wish to stand friendless and take your life into your own hands, then, of course, you are at liberty to do so."

The consul and the lawyer rose to go.

"One moment, Mr. Consul," Anders called after him. "Here I have drawn up my own defence, which I wish you and the gentleman here to read. It is in this way I wish to be defended."

He placed a large roll of paper on the table, and the two others hastened up to examine it. The lawyer, who was gazing at the opening page over the consul's shoulder, suddenly wheeled around upon his heel and burst into a ringing laugh. The consul, too, was obliged to smile at the curious English, while at the same time the primitive force and tremendous sincerity of the argument, not to speak of the entire absence of legal form, moved him to mingled admiration and pity.

"My dear Mr. Rustad," he said, "it will never do to present this document."

"Yes, yes, it will," cried Mr. Runyon, gayly, snatching up the paper and putting it into his pocket. "By means of this document I shall establish, beyond the shadow of a doubt, the fact of my client's insanity, before judge and jury, and I will bet against heavy odds, if any one has a mind to take me up."

And the lawyer, still greatly amused, dragged the consul with him through the open door, leaving the Norseman alone with the jailer.

VII.

The day for the trial arrived; Anders's arraignment of society in the person of Mr. Melville was read by his counsel, and excited much merriment among the lawyers and astonishment among the jurymen. The quaint phraseology and occasional misapplication of English words called forth peals of laughter; and in spite of the judge's endeavor to maintain order, he was sometimes obliged to relax his stern judicial mien into something resembling a smile. Thus, when the defendant spoke of "the beards of adversity" for "the barbs of adversity," and described the deceased bank president as having been "perforated with moral rottenness," while walking in the "slimy paths of perfidy," the court must have been more than human to conquer its disposition to laugh.

Anders sat pale and defiant in the prisoner's box, but gradually, as the laughter became

247

more frequent, a look of helpless perplexity settled upon his features. He was passionately convinced of being in the right, and if the world was out of gear, it was the world that was ridiculous, and not he. His gaze was fixed with anxious intensity on the faces of the twelve jurymen, to whom, as representatives of the American people, a peculiar sanctity attached. He had a dim notion that they had been elected for the purpose of trying him by the suffrage of the whole nation, very much as are the President and the Vice-President. They, he hoped, would be superior to this undignified merry-making; they would see clearly the justice of his cause, and the dishonesty and insolence of the lawyer who was trying to prove him insane. He saw them retire in order to deliberate; but hardly five minutes had elapsed before they all reappeared, and one of them, who seemed to be stouter and redder than the rest, addressed the judge in a pompous voice, declaring the prisoner to be "not guilty."

"Not guilty"—no, to be sure he was not

guilty. It was Mr. Melville who was guilty, and it was a pity he was not here to be tried. Then, after all, there was a spark of right and justice remaining in the world. At that moment the consul and Mr. Runyon came rushing up to him with extended hands.

"Allow me to congratulate you, Mr. Rustad," said the consul. "You ought to thank this gentleman heartily for his able efforts in your behalf."

"You see, after all we managed to prove you insane," whispered the lawyer, facetiously, — "or rather, as I expected, you proved yourself to be insane without much assistance on my part."

Anders suddenly saw the logic of the situation. In pronouncing him "not guilty," the jury had merely excused his deed by declaring that he was not responsible for it; they had accepted Mr. Runyon's plea that he was insane. Heart-sick and miserable, he turned away, and under the escort of two policemen walked out of the court-room. It was too late in the day to make out his papers of discharge, and he was therefore conducted to a much roomier and more comfortable cell, where he was only to spend the night. He flung himself on the bed, and motioned to the policemen to leave him alone. He felt as if something had snapped within him like the spring in a watch, and left the vital machinery hopelessly out of gear. He got up merely to try if he could hold himself erect, but his motions were those of an old man. All his confidence in his strength had deserted him. Presently his head began to swim, and a vapor gathered before his eyes. He let himself sink down again upon the couch.

Ten days later,—it was one of those early days in May when earth and sky seem to be united in one joyous harmony,—a peasant woman, in Norse costume, called at the Tombs, and inquired for Anders Rustad. She was carrying a chubby little boy, about eighteen months old, on her arm. She smoothed the child's hair carefully with her hand, while waiting for the reply of the door-keeper.

"Anders Rustad," she said, with anxious

inquiry in her voice and eyes. "Anders Rustad."

"Anders Rustad is pretty low to-day," said a man who had been summoned by the door-keeper. "He can't see nobody."

The young woman shook her head with a puzzled air. She did not understand. For three days she kept returning, and at last seated herself patiently on the curb-stone, waiting to be admitted. Whenever the gate was opened, she rushed forward and cried:

"Anders Rustad! Anders Rustad!"

But she received no reply. It was toward evening on the fourth day that the consul, accompanied by a physician, stepped from his *coupé* in front of the prison. Seeing the peasant woman, whose Norse costume caught his eye, he addressed her and asked her who she was.

"Anders Rustad," she said; "Anders Rustad. He is my husband. This is my child and his."

The consul beckoned to her to follow him, and she kept close to his heels while they mounted the stairs and walked through the long and gloomy galleries.

They stopped before the door of a cell, which was promptly opened. A dim lamp burned on a dirty-looking table, and there was a strong odor of kerosene in the room. Anders lay outstretched, pale and calm, on the iron bed. There was a pained resignation visible in his features, across which flickered now and then a fleeting gleam of a thought.

"Here is your wife, Mr. Rustad," said the consul, leading the woman up to the bedside. "And here is your little son."

The sick man turned his eyes in a tired, spiritless fashion, and fixed them upon his wife and child. The same puzzled look which, except in his moments of defiance, had of late become habitual with him, slowly contracted his brow, and he seemed to be struggling with some remote memory. The woman, too, seemed half-frightened, as if doubtful whether this haggard man, with the terrible eyes and unkempt beard and hair, could really be the strong and cheerful husband who, but a year ago, had gone out into the world to prepare a home for her. She stood for a while anxiously scrutinizing his features, then retired step by step toward the door, holding the child firmly clasped in her embrace.

"This is not my husband," she said to the consul, struggling with her tears, which were in her voice rather than in her eyes. "But I am going out to seek him."

"This is Anders Rustad," said the consul; "and if you are his wife, this is your last chance to bid him farewell in this world."

The woman once more drew near to the bed, gazed once more, and shuddered. The child began to cry piteously, and, hushing it at her bosom, she hastened out of the room.

"That was his wife," said the consul to the physician.

"Poor thing!" sighed the latter; "she did not know him."

He stooped down to feel the sick man's pulse. "He is sinking rapidly," he whispered. "It will be over soon."

"Do you know what caused his death, doctor ? " asked the consul, after a long pause, just as the last spark of life seemed to be flickering in the stiffening features.

" No," said the doctor.

" It was the over-development of a virtue His sense of justice killed him."

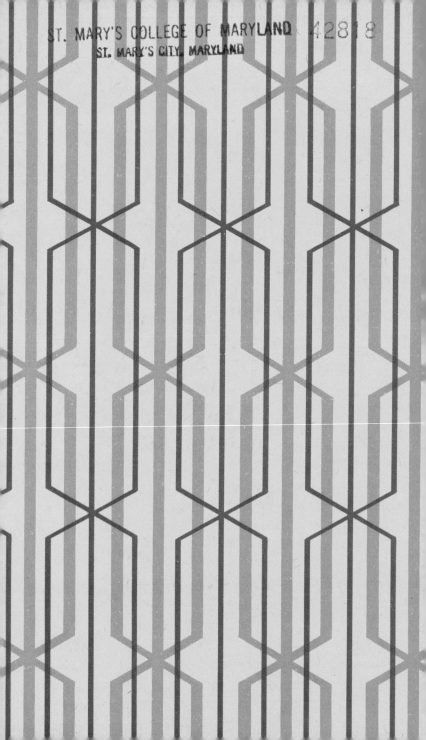